The Life and Fantastical "Crimes" of Spring-Heeled Jack

Being a Faithful Memoir of the Curious Youthful Adventures of Sir John Cecil Ashton, Once Known as "Spring Heeled Jack", Recounted by Himself

Fay ce que voudras

Foreword to the 1951 Edition
by Sir Edward Ashton

A few words may be required to introduce this new publication of my late grandfather's memoir, which he originally compiled just prior to the outbreak of the First World War and which has remained within our family since that time. My sister Emily and myself have very fond memories of our mother reading it aloud by lamplight, one chapter each night, during the early 1920s.

The name "Spring Heeled Jack" has recently returned to public attention via the actor Tod Slaughter's revival of the old Victorian melodrama, in which "Jack" is somewhat conflated with a certain other, distinctly nefarious "Jack" who haunted the streets of Whitechapel during the 1880s. Although, upon reflection, perhaps it was "Jack the Ripper" who borrowed from the name and mystique of "Spring Heeled Jack"! In any case, the aptly-named Mr. Slaughter has long portrayed the latter character on our London and provincial stages, and most recently in a "tele-play" produced by the British Broadcasting Corporation.

The villainous "Jack" also made an appearance on the silver screen several years ago, in "The Curse of the Wraydons", although - rather disappointingly - he failed to take so much as an ordinary leap, never mind the spectacular bounds one so associates with the Spring Heeled Jack of Victorian times.

Underlying all of these portrayals, however, has been the assumption that Spring Heeled Jack was an out-and-out malefactor. That's rather rankled within our family, for reasons that shall, we trust, become apparent to readers of this memoir, which we are now pleased to present to the public for the first time.

Edward Ashton
London
1951

Preface: to my children

(by Sir John Cecil Ashton - undated, but circa July of 1913)

My writing of this memoir has been prompted by Isobel's recent question about the motto of our family crest, and about what prompted me to change it so many years ago.

It seems to me well past time that these matters should be laid forth, for what insight or enjoyment they might avail to all of you, and perhaps, should you wish, for future publication and thus general posterity; although, undesirous of the public's attention in this matter, your mother and myself should appreciate it if you'd wait until we've both passed on (and don't worry, there's still some life in us yet!)

After some deliberation, I've chosen to employ, to some extent, the style of the epistolary novelist, in part so that I might incorporate certain newspaper clippings and sketches that have been quietly yellowing away in my cabinet for the past forty years or thereabouts. Most of these ephemera were first collected by a boon comrade of my youthful days, whose name and legacy I shall present herein, and I should very much appreciate it if they might be preserved in any more formal edition of this memoir.

Now, past adventures await anew - but where to begin?

Chapter 1

When, finally, my last rites had been read and the entire macabre ritual of shuffling priests and prurient bureaucrats had been played, I was ordered to stand. It is my shameful duty to record that I could not. It is one thing to prepare for battle, even against Sikh warriors, and quite another to know with certainty that you have less than one hour to live.

Indignity and naked fear had stunned my senses and numbed my muscles, and this seemed no news to the burly turn-keys who hauled me roughly to my feet and held me upright between them. The other men filed out of the cell and, supported by a man at either elbow, wrists and ankles shackled, I found myself shuffling after them into the galley.

Convicted and condemned, a filthy prisoner in the bowels of Newgate Gaol …

My thoughts were vastly scattered, a confusion of memories, most clearly that of a terrible dream of freedom that I had so recently suffered, but also of training at Aldershot Camp, the notice of my father's death, the serene face of Guru Alli … and, most vividly, cousin Roland's placid treachery as he bore false witness against me.

At the same time, I fantasized about escape. I could wrench free of the man on my left who, though not lacking in size, seemed mostly fat, then drive my elbow sharply into his wind … but at that very thought his grip tightened upon my arm and he glanced meaningfully at his colleague. I sensed with certainty that these men knew every trick, every ruse that might be conjured by a desperate man, and that they were well prepared to counter each and every one.

We arrived in the Press Yard, still deeply shadowed of a winter's morning, to be met by the Sheriff, the Chaplain and some other men. I was scarce aware of any of them, though, my full attention – seemingly more focussed now than at any other moment in my life – being drawn to the tall, thin figure standing apart from them – the hooded man in black. I was suddenly overcome with a superstitious dread, which seemed to surge up through my body from the frozen soil beneath my thin prisoner's shoes. I cried out and my knees gave way again. Every fibre of my very being feared this faceless man, who embodied the fact of my imminent death.

"I am innocent! For the love of God above, you must believe me!"

The sheriff motioned with his right hand and one of the others started forward, a man with a terribly pock-marked face. He secured a wide leather belt about my waist and the men to either side unshackled my hands and then forced them into two stiff and sturdy leather cuffs positioned over each thigh. Some hard bundle dug into the small of my back. Pock-face proceeded to strap my wrists tight into the cuffs, murmuring something that might have been "all be over soon."

A voice inside my mind inquired as to the advantage of this contraption over the standard shackles to which I had become accustomed and another part replied that this was to prevent me from grabbing at the rope when the moment came. At this thought, the yard grew suddenly dark and foggy, as if pervaded by a pea-souper, and I have no further memory of being dragged towards my doom through the shadowed alleyways of Newgate Gaol.

The shock of frigid wind and unaccustomed sunlight revived me from my swoon, and I found myself standing atop a wooden platform, a good eight feet above the pavement.

The ankle cuffs and chains were gone from my feet but, of course, both turn-keys still stood at my sides, their arms entwined through mine. There, a few feet ahead, stood the struts that supported the gallows beams and a single noose, all lightly rimed with hoar-frost. It took a mighty effort to wrench my gaze from that sight, but somehow I managed the feat. Beyond and below, I could see the large and bustling crowd that had gathered to bear witness to this morning's entertainment. Many wore bright colours and there were numerous women and children amongst the throng.

I heard the calls of a pedlar hawking roasted chestnuts and another offering copies of the Newgate Gazette. In the same benumbed state I found myself shunted forward, still half-supported by the warders on either side, and heard a swell of hissing from the crowd below. I had read that much money was wagered on the behaviour of condemned men on their way to the gallows. Never, in a thousand, thousand years, would I have dreamed that, one day, I should be the subject of such betting.

"Up! Stand up and be a man, damn you," muttered the warder to my right. Perhaps he had some shillings on my performance. I did my damndest, indeed: by some enormous act of a scattered will, forcing my legs to straighten, to bear my own weight. Absurdly, I resolved to imagine that I was back on the parade ground, with the same clean-limbed officer's bearing that had been the pride of my late, lamented father.

We passed quite close to the crowd at this point, and some urchin pegged a piece of rotten fruit, which missed me and splattered against the brick wall. I found myself momentarily fascinated by its dripping yellow ooze, knowing that I would be departed from this world before it froze into hard gum.

The Chaplain then stepped forward and commenced his prayer. I was not moved to join him. Instead, I stared out into space, my gaze meeting the building opposite the scaffold, where I noticed well-to-do looking gentlemen and their ladies peering out from every window. They looked warm and in high spirits.

The Chaplain had ceased his droning and a cry went up from the crowd in the street, "Hats off!" I understood this to be no gesture of respect, but simply a demand that the men to the front should remove their headwear so that those behind would be afforded an unimpeded view as I dropped through the trap. I knew that below the platform stood a high barrier, to spare the audience the sight of my final moments.

The fearsome figure of the executioner now loomed before me, and again I felt faint. Calling upon every reserve, I remained standing as if to attention. I was vaguely aware of the crowd's muttering. It began to snow, white flakes spotting the executioner's black vestements and his terrible hood. The tall man then moved behind me and the turn-keys stepped away.

At that moment, there was a commotion in the crowd. A young woman, perhaps a bawd, her arms muffled in a red woolen shawl, fell into hysterics, screaming and trying to scramble over the railing separating the throng from the scaffold tower. I felt a cold line traced straight up the middle of my back, from my waist to the nape of my neck.

The woman was quickly restrained and hushed by others in the crowd, and her despairing face was the last thing I saw before a white linen hood was drawn over my head, quickly followed by the noose. As it was drawn tight from behind, the rough hemp prickled against my neck through the cloth.

At this, the crowd became hushed. I felt snow alight upon my helpless hands as gentle as kisses and dreaded the ignominy of dying so, wrongfully accused and convicted, now trussed and blindfolded. I believe that a single, hot tear rolled down my cheek, then chilled and turned to ice.

And then I spoke aloud inside that victim's hood;

"I vow before God or the Devil, whichever will hear me; that if there be power in Heaven or Hell to afford me revenge, I will make them pay. I will make them pay for this!"

There was a sharp sound and the floor dropped from beneath my feet. I fell, not far, and felt the noose tighten. I tasted blood. I could not force my jaws open and the pressure in my head was terrible, terrible. A rushing sound filled my ears. I felt my legs kicking out, my arms straining desperately against the leather cuffs, hands clenching into fists, blood bubbling from between my lips. My nostrils flared, sucking for breath that was not there, too late, too late … the whiteness before my eyes faded to gray, to red and then to black.

Chapter 2

The Trial for High Treason
of
Captain John Cecil "Jack" Ashton.

The trial took place at the Central Criminal Court, on Thursday, the 9th of July, 1865, before Lord Denman, Mr Baron Alderson and Mr Justice Patteson.

The indictment was in the following terms:--

"Central Criminal Court, to wit.-- The jurors for our lady the Queen, upon their oath present, that John Cecil Ashton, known to his acquaintances as "Jack" Ashton, aged twenty-seven years, late of Ashton Hall, Guildford, in the county of Surrey, former Captain of the Bengal Lancers, son of the late Sir Cecil Geoffrey Ashton, being a subject and soldier of our lady the Queen, heretofore, to wit, on the 10th of June, in the year of our Lord 1865, within the jurisdiction of the said court, as a false traitor to our lady the Queen, maliciously and traitorously, with force and arms, etc., did compass, imagine, and intend to bring and put our said lady the Queen and Prince Albert to death.

To this indictment the prisoner pleaded not guilty.

The prosecution was conducted by the Attorney-General, the Solicitor-General, Sir F. Pollock, Mr Adolphus, Mr Wightman and Mr Gurney; and Mr Sidney Taylor and Mr Bodkin appeared for the defence.

The court was crowded to excess by persons of distinction during the two days occupied by the trial.

The Attorney-General opened the case to the jury, and in the course of his address he said:

"The prisoner at the bar is a young man of twenty-seven years. He was born, as I understand, at Guildford, to the house of the late and esteemed Sir Cecil Ashton. His mother, the Lady Margaret Ashton, died of the consumption when he was four years old. The prisoner was educated at Cambridge and then as a cavalry officer at Aldershot Camp. He was reported by his Sergeant, Edward Burrage, to have excelled in his studies, most particularly in the areas of tactics, explosives, gymnastics and riding.

Gentlemen, it would appear that, while stationed with the Queen's Lancers in India, where had given every appearance of performing model service as an officer, the defendant secretly formed and matured a plan to make an attempt upon the life of the Sovereign. The Court has received documents signed by the defendant, in the form of diary entries and letters to anonymous fellow conspirators, whose names he has refused to reveal, detailing the scope and nature of this treasonous plot.

These documents were supplied to the police by the defendant's cousin, Roland Ashton, who had intercepted them while the defendant was travelling by ship to England from India. I should explain that the defendant had been released from his military duties by his commanding officer, Colonel Eustace Manfred, so that he might pay his final respects to his late father and thereafter assume his responsibilities as heir to the Ashton estates.

Upon his ship's arrival at Victoria Dock, the defendant was met by a deputation of police constables, who attempted to place him under arrest. He then endeavoured to escape from the constables' lawful custody, breaking the nose of one of them in a scuffle and throwing another bodily into the Thames, before their colleagues overpowered him, forcing him to halt his escape and to submit to being clapped in darbies. The prisoner was then taken to the station-house at Victoria Cross, where he was held overnight before transportation to Newgate Prison, where he has been held since.

The documents provided as evidence by Roland Ashton reveal a plot of the most pernicious and base form of anarchism and treason and date back to the 4th of May, in the present year. These documents have been copied for inspection by the officers of this Court.

You are probably aware that it is the custom of her Majesty Queen Victoria, since she has been united with Prince Albert, frequently to take the afternoon or evening air in the parks without any military escort, and with the simplicity of private life. This custom was well known to all her loyal subjects, and indeed to the whole community. As is detailed in the documents provided, it was the defendant's intention to bury an explosive device along the path followed by Her Majesty's carriage. This device was to have been triggered by means of a trip-wire when the carriage passed between two trees.

It will appear that these documents were brought to the station-house and shown to the prisoner, who stated that the papers did not belong to him, and that he had no knowledge of their origin. A constable was then dispatched to search the contents of the defendant's luggage on board the ship. Here were found concealed additional copies of the documents, likewise in the defendant's hand, and also sketches detailing the precise construction of the explosive device, along with a map of the routes followed by Her Majesty's carriage through the parks. The prisoner again denied all knowledge of these documents and claimed not to know how they had come to be concealed in his luggage.

Under these circumstances, gentlemen, if the prisoner is accountable for his acts, will you say whether there is any reasonable doubt of his guilt? It appears to me that if the prisoner was at the time accountable for his actions, there can be no such doubt.

I now come to the question whether the prisoner was accountable for his actions at the time when the offence was committed. And I will at once admit, under the law of England, that if he was then of unsound mind - if at the time when that act was committed he was afflicted with insanity, he will be entitled to be acquitted on that ground. I must say that, so far as I have yet learned, there is no reason to believe that the prisoner at the time he committed this crime was in a state of mind which takes away his criminal responsibility for the conspiracy to commit Regicide."

The evidence for the prosecution was then gone through in corroboration of the statements of the learned Attorney-General, and Mr Sidney Taylor addressed the jury for the defence. Having argued upon the facts of the case proved by the witnesses for the prosecution, upon which he proceeded to the important issue of insanity. It was not the first time, unhappily, that a conspiracy had arisen to take away the life of the Sovereign of this country; but Mr. Taylor rejoiced to say, for the sake of our national character, that in no one instance had such an act been done by a person possessing a sane mind.

A body of evidence was then adduced with a view to supporting the defence of insanity which was set up. Medical witnesses provided by the prosecution were also examined, who gave their decided opinion that the prisoner was in a sound state of mind.

Lord Denman summed up the evidence, and at the end of the second day's trial the jury returned a verdict rejecting the insanity defence and convicting the prisoner of High Treason. He was ordered to be detained during her Majesty's pleasure, and was subsequently conveyed again to Newgate Jail, there to await justice in the form of hanging by the neck until dead.

Chapter 3

I awoke to pain, pitch blackness and a sound.

A scraping noise.

From the pressure on the base of my skull and across my shoulders and hips, I could tell that I was lying upon my back. My fingertips told me that I lay upon rough wooden boards. I could not tell whether my eyes were opened or closed. There was an abominably harsh pain in my throat, my mouth was full of something foul and it hurt to breathe. I forced my jaws open and spat out a lump of congealed blood and a small part of my tongue. I heard it strike something just over my face, and felt it land beside my ear.

I woke again to the sound of my own strangled screams, in the grip of a nightmare of having been buried alive and found that it was so. Blood dripped onto my face, into my eyes, from the splintered nubs of my fingernails as they clawed at the lid of the coffin. I beat my fists and kicked against the walls. From somewhere above, there was a scraping sound. In a moment of terrible clarity, I knew that something had gone wrong with the hanging. I had been rendered senseless, perhaps terribly wounded, but not killed. There were men above, shoveling dirt onto my coffin.

I redoubled my kicking and beating, doing my utmost to cry out to them, but the confines of the walls and lid offered me no space to exert my blows and all that escaped my lips was a gargling wheeze. My throat felt as if I had swallowed fire and I could not lift my head at all, not one inch.

Exhausted, agonised and despairing, I lay still, hearing only the thundering of my heart, the soft clicking and whistling of each contorted breath, and the muffled voices and scraping efforts of the men above me. But wait – surely the sounds of the outside world should be growing quieter and not louder?
Steeling myself against pain, hope and reason, I committed to making all the noise I was able to. I smashed my fists raw against the walls, drummed my bare heels bloody against the floor, and cried out with every ounce of will, if very little voice – "Help me! Help me, I am alive!"

And so I was when seconds, minutes or hours later, the lid was wrenched from the box and I found myself staring up into a rectangle of starry sky. A silhouette, presumably the face of one of my saviours, moved across my field of vision, and then I was blinded by light from a shuttered lantern. Utterly exhausted, I could do nothing but lie still, eyes closed against the glare, and breathe in the sweet, cold air.

" 'e's gorn mad!" The guttural whisper was yet music to my ears.

"Wouldn't you? Poor devil …" his companion replied, in a heavy Scotts burr.

"Look at the state of 'im. Can 'e 'ear us, d'you think?"

"Gawd knows."

I heard and felt a heavy thump as one of the men slid into the hole and landed on the edges of the coffin, a foot braced to either side. He bent forwards and murmured, "Ye're safe for now, be we gots to move yer quick and quiet, d'ye ken?" I tried to reply but could force no further sound from my ravaged throat. The Scott turned to his confederate. "He's mute, but he's alive, at least. Give me a hand."

I have no memory of being pulled from my grave, nor of the faces of these two men. Nor do I recall being loaded into the carriage upon whose floor I later found myself, my body a jigsaw of bone-deep aches, stinging pain and numbness, unable even to lift my head to peer through a window. I believe that I had travelled several miles before the rocking of the carriage sent me off into a mercifully dreamless sleep.

Chapter 4

When next I opened my eyes, I was lying on a cot in a close, windowless, oak-panelled room, dimly lit by an oil lantern. For one horrible instant, I wondered if my rescue had been merely another cruel dream; whether I was still a prisoner in my cell and that the execution had not yet taken place. But, no – as I lifted my hands to my face I saw that their many wounds had been dressed and two fingers splinted, and I could feel another bandage and perhaps a poultice about my throat. The beard that had been allowed to grow out at Newgate was gone, but I bore a tidy moustache. I was wearing a clean convalescent's night shift.

Painfully, slowly, I turned my head a few inches and saw a bottle of water resting atop a small table beside the cot. I tried to raise myself up, but I must have strained every muscle in my exertions to escape the coffin, and I could scarcely move.

"You're awake, Sir?" A cultured man's voice from the darkness beyond the reach of the candle's light. He stepped forward and I beheld a short, heavily set gentleman of advanced years, dressed elegantly, his expression unreadable behind his moustaches.

"It's all right, I understand that you cannot speak. That shall be dealt with in good time. For the moment, we must concentrate on your general recuperation."

The fellow very gently raised my head and poured a little water into my mouth.

"Swallow slowly and carefully, Sir, and please make no attempt to speak. That's very good."

The water slaked the fire in my throat and loosened some of the dried blood that had caked the insides of my lips. I almost gagged, but managed to relax and the spasm dwindled. He offered me a handkerchief and I spat into it as discreetly as possible under the circumstances.

"Very good, Sir. Now, I know that you will have many questions, but I'm afraid that it is not my place to answer them. I can tell you, sincerely, that no harm will come to you here and that I shall do my utmost to bring you back to good health, just as quickly as possible. Try to sleep again, now."

He left quietly through a door that opened just enough to suggest the flicker of firelight beyond, and I wondered whether I was ensconced in an antechamber, perhaps adjacent to the living room of some wealthy family's country manor.

The next period passed in a delirium punctuated with horrific nightmares. In the most vivid, I seemed to re-live the horror of being called into the office of Colonel Manfred back in Bangalore, there to receive the devastating news that my dear father had died some days before. The Colonel had, in reality, been tender with me then, arranging immediately to discharge me from my duties and assisting with the organisation of my passage back to England.

In the delirium, though, I reeled away from this appalling news, seeming to stumble from his office straight into the hands of the constables at Victoria Dock; they spun me about and suddenly I was shackled at the bar of the Old Bailey, and there was my cousin Roland, in the vestments of the chief judge, condemning me to hang …

The doctor would shake me awake from such black fantasies and assure me that I was safe and on the mend. I progressed from taking sips of water to drinking a nourishing, meaty broth. He would change the dressings on my hands and feet, apply a fresh poultice to my wounded throat, keep the lantern aglow and discreetly assist me with the necessities of sanitation. He also applied a salve and bandages to a narrow graze that seemed to run the length of my spine, which I had no memory of having received.

Eventually, perhaps after the passage of a several days – between the fact that the room was windowless and my frequent naps, I had no real way of judging the passage of time - I became able to order my thoughts and could comfortably raise myself into a sitting position, though I had to support my head with one hand in doing so, for the muscles of my neck were still strained and weak. At this point, unbidden, the doctor provided me with a stronger light and with some books to pass the time. He politely refused to give me his name.

Bed-ridden by the injuries I had done my feet in trying to escape the coffin and still awfully frail, my mind was yet a-fever with questions and speculations, and I tried to order the facts as they seemed to be.

Roland had forged papers damning me as a traitor, obviously so that he could assume control over my Father's estates, for he was next in the line of succession. Somehow, perhaps by bribing the constable charged with searching my luggage, or even one of the sailors aboard ship, he had contrived to have further false evidence planted there; this, in combination with the fictitious plot being cleverly tailored to my military expertise, had been enough to convince the jury of my guilt. The only penalty for conspiracy to commit Regicide was execution by hanging, but by some miracle of God or trick of the Devil, the executioner had failed in his appointed task.

Who were they who had dug me from my grave, and how on Earth had they known that I was alive in the first place? The thought crossed my mind that they might have been grave robbers, but no – I distinctly recalled their conversation and they had shown no sign of surprise at finding me alive. They had seemed men on a mission. So, were they acting on their own behalf, or upon the orders of another? If another, then that party must somehow have known that I had survived the noose.

Further, although I remembered fragments of the carriage ride, I had no idea how long I might have travelled whilst insensible, nor in which direction. What day was it? Was I even still in the vicinity of London? This led naturally to the question of whose philanthropy I owed for the doctor's care. I surmised that the same benefactor who had arranged my rescue and transport must also be responsible for my present care and lodgings. Was it the doctor himself? He spoke little enough as it was, but from his words when I had first awoken, it was my impression that he, too, was acting on behalf of a third party.

When next the doctor came to attend me, he brought a new unguent which he assured me would help my swollen throat, as I was still unable to speak above a hoarse whisper. As usual, he politely deflected my questions and concentrated on my recuperation. The wounds to my tongue, hands and feet were now healing nicely and I spent some considerable time massaging and flexing my muscles back into condition. Perhaps another day or two passed before I could stand unassisted – my feet had been badly scraped and bruised black and blue, but fortunately not broken - and then manage more than a few hobbling steps. At last, I could begin to think about exploring beyond the confines of my invalid's room. I'd had quite enough of confined spaces.

Upon the doctor's next visit, he found me sitting on the bed and practicing a yogic posture while reading a book.

"Now Sir, you are convalescing very well indeed, to tie yourself up in such knots! That is an Indian exercise, is it not?" He placed a bundle on the table beside my cot.

"It is," I whispered. I had found that as long as I did not engage my vocal cords, I could make myself understood quite clearly.

"Fascinating people, the Hindoo. I have great respect for some of their medicine. I assume that you learned this calisthenic business from a native master?"

"A man named Guru Alli, a genius at wrestling and physical culture. He was attached to my regiment in Bangalore."

"Excellent, I'm quite sure that his lessons have speeded your recovery. Now, again I must apologise for having kept you in the dark, so to speak, regarding your whereabouts and other matters. I have now been authorised to offer you passage to those who will be happy to answer your questions. If you would dress, and then follow me … ?" The Doctor stepped out of the room.

Curiosity fairly bursting, I eagerly did as bidden, donning the clothes and boots that he had brought in, and strode out the door with as much alacrity as was possible under the circumstances. However, what I saw when I left that room fairly sucked the wind from my newly-filled sails.

I had clearly been far off the mark in imagining a country manor; in fact, I had been convalescing in a wood-panelled antechamber within some kind of underground cavern.

I found myself in what was evidently a man-made tunnel, white chalk-stone walls illuminated by the glow of a single fiery torch which the doctor extracted from it's resting place in an iron brazier. The sheer incongruity of this sober, cultured man bearing such a Medieval implement almost caused me to laugh aloud, but I dared not, caring neither to offend him nor to damage my still-fragile vocal cords. So I followed meekly a few steps behind the doctor, down this low-ceilinged passageway, towards my appointment with unknown destiny.

Soon we came upon a vast circular chamber whose ceiling was so high that it was beyond the reach of the doctor's torch, and thus entirely invisible to me. The walls, though, were decorated with opulent tapestries depicting various mythological scenes. The doctor marched resolutely through and I had but a moment to take in any detail in the torchlight. One hanging appeared to portray the Biblical Adam and Eve; another, the Scandinavian trickster-deity Loki astride a flying boar; a third, barely glimpsed, might have been a depiction of one of Dante's nine circles of Hell. We passed by a gleaming wooden pole supporting a darkly colourful pennant, which bore the motto "*Fay ce que voudras*", richly embroidered in gleaming golden thread. I recognised the French – "Do as thou wilt."

Passing through a doorway almost directly opposite that through which we had entered, we made our way down a very long passage whose walls were decorated with the faces of ghosts, skulls and all manner of imps, crudely carved into the chalk. My heart beat faster due to the unaccustomed exercise and the sheer excitement of this adventure. Who had created this phantasmagoric underworld, and to what purpose?

We moved on in silence through other chambers, all curiously shaped, decorated and furnished. One was ovular and contained a number of artificial stalagmites, garishly lit in bright colours. The next was perfectly circular and somberly illuminated by a large stained glass window which reminded me of that of the Ashton Hall chapel, except that the light for this one seemed to be provided by candles or lanterns set into the wall behind it. I could vaguely make out statuettes in various lewd poses, stationed in the alcoves that ringed the walls. Idly, I wondered just how far beneath the surface of the ground we might be.

The next tunnel led into a triangular cavern whose ceiling was hung with many brass bells of various sizes, and whose floor was thickly padded with what appeared to be the pelts of bears, goats and red deer. Finally, as we emerged into yet another chamber, this one brilliantly lit by numerous coloured lanterns and decorated as might have befit a gentlemen's club of the previous century, the doctor paused and passed his torch to me.

"This is as far as I am able to take you. The answers that you seek are down the next passage. I wish you the best of luck and health, young Sir."

I had no time to question him as he courteously motioned me to proceed. As I was about to exit, though, I turned and looked him in the eye.

"I believe that I owe you my life, Doctor. Please consider me forever in your debt." My voice came out as a sibilant whisper, an unintentional piece of melodrama amplified by the echo of the cavern, and we both smiled a little.

"Doctor?" he replied, still smiling. "Wherever did you get that idea?" And then, pausing only to extract and light another torch, he was gone back the way we had come.

Stooping low to gain entry and hunching over to shield my torch against water dripping from the lintel, I passed through the opening and came across perhaps the strangest sight yet. The next chamber was bisected by a broad stream of dark water, perhaps twenty feet across, that emerged from around a bend to my left and continued around another to the right.

A shallow wooden skiff leant neatly against the wall at my side, and a guide rope stretched across from an iron hook embedded in the wall at head height to another on the opposite shore. I was half-expecting Charon himself to emerge from the gloom and demand a coin in payment, but no, this crossing was evidently up to me.

I could see no means to perform this task while holding the torch and there appeared to be no convenient way to lodge it upright in the skiff, so I carefully set it down on the chalk bank, propped up against the wall. My bruised hands were just up to the task of lifting the boat and positioning it half into the water, whose smooth current was both surprisingly strong and exceedingly cold.

Bracing the boat with my foot and trusting that I could always return to the previous chamber for a lantern should the torch be extinguished, I retrieved it and lobbed it across the stream to the opposite bank. It spun in flight, casting bizarre shadows upon an already bizarre scene, and bounced off the opposite wall, but the fire survived its flight over water.

I did not fancy a ducking in that swift, dark stream, especially in that I did not know what was around the next bend, and so took care to balance myself well upon the skiff before pulling out. Between the current and my injured hands I had a time of it manoeuvering across, and I was now sweating freely with the exertion, but there was no incident and within a few moments I was safe and dry on the opposite bank. Steeling myself to expect nothing and yet be ready for anything, I stepped into what I devoutly hoped was the final chamber.

Chapter 5

I entered to find myself standing before an upholstered stool in a candle-lit chamber whose walls were draped with red satin. Beyond the stool stood a crescent of five high-backed wooden chairs, almost thrones, in which sat five men dressed in dark formal suits and ties. They gave every appearance of conservative propriety except for their extraordinary masks, which might have been crafted for a rural Mummer's play.

"I'm so glad that you're feeling better. Might I offer you some tea?" The man who had spoken was seated in the farthest chair to my left, and was wearing a brown-furred domino mask replete with weasel-like snout and whiskers. I shook my head warily.

"Abbot Holt, Brothers Farmara, Vinegar Tom and Sacke?"

Murmured assents from two of them, a shake of the head from a large fellow in a bull's face and horns, who already had a mug, and a courteous "No, thank you, Brother Newes" from an elderly-sounding gentleman wearing the face of an albino cat, who sat in the second to last chair.

"Brother Newes" poured tea and I wondered whether I had gone irretrievably mad.

Next spoke a trim man in the guise of a black rabbit, who was seated next to Newes. I could not tell whether his moustache was his own, or a feature of his mask. His voice, like the other two whom had spoken thus far, was cultured.

"Straight down to business, then, Sir. We understand that your throat has not fully recovered from your recent ordeal, so we shall do our best to anticipate your questions. You might care to take a seat," and he nodded towards an upholstered stool set before the assembly. I sat and waited.

"Firstly, you will no doubt be wondering where you are. Other than our identities, that is amongst the few secrets that we shall, regretfully, be keeping from you for the time being. I do apologise, but this is a matter of long-standing protocol within our Order. Incidentally, you may think of me as Brother Sacke."

Their "Order" – some form of Freemasonry, then? Sacke's voice sounded lawyerly …

"Secondly, we are aware of the situation vis-à-vis your father's tragic death, his estate, and the role played by your cousin in your conviction and imprisonment. In brief, we know a very great deal about you, young Sir. I trust that you will forgive my familiarity."

Brother Sacke sipped at his tea and my mind reeled at the import of his words – if these men knew the truth, then they could clear my name, expose Roland's perfidy … but this train of thought was interrupted by the heavy-set, bull-masked man sitting next to him, in the central chair.

"I'm Brother Vinegar Tom. Thirdly, and Christ knows it's taken enough doing, if you'll pardon me French, we are they who 'appen to have saved your life a week's past at Newgate. The h'execution was a sham – we greased some palms, 'ad others replaced, and 'ad you fitted with a gimmick 'arness at the moment of truth. The belt around your waist took most of the strain an' it kept you alive."

A memory - as the young woman in the Newgate crowd had screamed, I recalled the sensation of a cold line being drawn up my back, beneath my shirt and jacket. A cord, or cable, had been hidden in the waist-restraint until that moment! It would have been a simple matter to hook such a contraption to some concealed eyelet in the hangman's rope, whilst the crowd's attention was on the commotion in front. I grinned at the sheer deviltry of it, but I was yet quite off-balance and yearned to learn more.

"The h'executioner was in our pay, as was 'is 'umble assistant and the 'ore down in the crowd. We also 'ad a man 'iding in the box beneath, ready to 'old you up if need be – didn't quite come to that but your neck ended up takin' a bit more of the noose than planned. You were away with the fairies after a minute or so. It were touch and go, I can tell you that for nuffink." He paused to clear his throat. "Then we 'ad you dug up, of course, and you know the rest of that side."

Brother Vinegar Tom looked to his left, where sat the man in the white-furred cat's mask.

"Bringing you up to date, Sir, except for the crucial matter of 'why?' Oh, excuse me; for present purposes, if it should please you to address me, my title is Abbot Holt.

The answer as to "why" is a little involved. We five, and another of like number, style ourselves the Hellfire Club. You have probably heard the stories of Dashwood and his merry rakes, their orgies and cod-Satanism, a century ago. It is common knowledge that the Club disbanded in Seventeen Sixty-Three, and long may it remain so."

"Too right!" interjected Brother Vinegar Tom.

"However, the truth is that we did not disband at all, merely factionalised and, I should say, diversified. The present Club, of which I have the honour to be President, maintains certain interests – political, religious, philosophical, financial, and so-forth – here and throughout the Empire. At times we have been of some service to certain other parties, where their concerns have co-incided with our own. Your present concerns, Sir, happen to co-incide with ours, in a manner of speaking, and so here we find ourselves."

The "Abbot" spread his hands expansively.

"We find ourselves in need of a man without an identity, specifically yourself; but regrettably, we cannot yet reveal the nature of that need. You may wish to ask questions?"

The five of them sat silently, masks eerily illuminated in the flickering candle-light. Exerting my voice carefully, in something like a stage whisper, I began:

"I thank you for my life and am indebted to you all. But of course I do have an identity. You gentlemen can help me to prove my innocence, and that is the most important matter of all, from my point of view. Once I am re-established as the Lord of Ashton Hall I will be in a much better position to assist you, and so I shall, upon my word of honour."

Now spoke the man to Abbot Holt's left side, whose dress was more colourful than those of his companions and who wore a rather jolly mask representing some breed of dog – a spaniel, I guessed.

"Therein lies the rub, good fellow. I am Brother Farmara and I trust that your wounds are not too sore?"

"I'll not be turning cart-wheels in the near future, but I am recovering, thank you."

"Excellent. In the mean-time, I'm afraid that it falls to me to deliver the bad news. We shall not be assisting you in the matter of your false imprisonment, nor your claim to the Ashton estate. Jack Ashton is dead and gone."

Chapter 6

I rose from the stool, aflame with indignation, and suddenly became aware of a pistol in the hand of polecat-faced Brother Newes. Utterly flummoxed, I forced myself to sit down again. Other than the brute who called himself Vinegar Tom, these man – my saviours, my new captors? - were obviously educated, and perhaps one or two were even equal to me in social rank. I could make no sense of their actions, nor even guess as to their intentions.

"Why the deuce have you gone to such theatrical lengths to have me rescued and then turn around and refuse to expose Roland? What do you want from me?"

A cold rage began to seep into my stomach as I contemplated one very good reason.

"Is this blackmail?"

"No, young Sir," replied Brother Farmara. "Not a hundred miles from it, but no. The Hellfire Club is not entirely unscrupulous, but nor are we a philanthropic society. We are, after a fashion, mercenaries in an invisible war, and you are to be one of our key infantrymen. Temporarily, of course.

Abbot Holt has reminded you that you are now a man without an identity. Mark me, as far as anyone in England is concerned, Jack Ashton died upon the Newgate Gallows eight days past. If we were to dig into his unmarked grave, we would find the newly moldering remains of one Jack Ashton, or at least a reasonable facsimile."

"Very reasonable, Brother Farmara," said Vinegar Tom, whom I gathered to have taken charge of this phase of the operation. Farmara continued:

"Were you to present yourself and your story before any authority in the land, you would be taken for a charlatan at best, a lunatic at worst. Even if you could somehow prove that you are the man once known as Jack Ashton, that man has already been convicted of treason. You have nothing but the clothes upon your back, which, incidentally, have been provided to you courtesy of the Hellfire Club. You owe us your life, my dear boy."

I paused to take this in. I did, apparently, owe everything to this band of dangerous eccentrics. Now was not the moment to test the limits of whatever loyalty they expected from me.

"So I'm free to go?"

"We trust that you shall be, in due course. Once you have heard us out, Brother Vinegar Tom shall remove you from this place to another, where we have arranged comfortable and secure lodgings for you. Your continued health and well-being are of great import to us."

"And how long am I to remain a 'guest' of your Club?"

"I regret that we cannot tell. We are at a delicate stage of this operation. Perhaps a matter of weeks, perhaps some months. In any event, you will be well cared for until we have need to call upon you."

"And what will the Hellfire Club take as payment for my life?"

"All in good time. For the moment, we have been assured that you are well enough to make your start."

At this, the burly, bull-masked Vinegar Tom stood up. He was a real powerhouse, and I understood that there were to be no shenanigans between here and there, wherever either turned out to be.

"We trust, Sir, that you will think well on everything that we have told you," intoned the aged Abbot Holt, as his colleague led me from their company.

Chapter 7

The first hours of the long coach journey passed uneventfully. The cab's shutters were drawn, of course, and try as I might to gauge the location of the Hellfire Club's lair by subtle cues of light and sound, I was as lost as ever. I confess that I dozed a little off and on, the hulking, masked Brother Vinegar Tom offering no conversation whatsoever, although he freely shared some extra clothes against the chill: a woollen scarf and gloves, a jacket and some sturdy boots. He also offered food from a wicker hamper, a simple and hearty rural fare of soft dark bread, beef, cheese and beer. I was thus afforded ample time to consider the events of the past month.

Moments stood out in stark relief; the dreadful news of my father's passing, my failed flight from the law at Victoria Dock, my first sight of Newgate Gaol. My scaffold-vow against the sheer perfidy of cousin Roland. I recalled the unbridled panic of being buried alive and, fragmentarily, my recuperation under the Doctor's care. Vividly, I remembered the humiliation and despair of being imprisoned in a dank cell, of being fed twice daily through a hatch in the door.

Eventually, I knew by the slowing of the coach and the hub-bub going on outside that we were surrounded by people and coach traffic. I decided then and there that, despite whatever two-edged kindness had been offered by the Hellfire Club, I would be double-damned if I was going to spend another moment as anyone's prisoner.

Thus resolved, I lunged for the door and my left arm was immediately caught in a vice-like grip by Vinegar Tom, who moved with an astounding speed for a man of his size. I had no hope of matching his strength, but I had another trick in reserve, and with a sweep of my free arm I knocked his mask askew. With the eye-holes dislodged he was momentarily blinded, and at this chance I bit down hard into his clutching thumb.

The brute roared with pain and released my arm, and in a flash I was out the door, falling awkwardly and landing upon my forearms and knees. I was completely dazzled by the sudden brightness of daylight and felt snow-dusted cobblestones beneath my hands. I stumbled away from where I reckoned the carriage to be, buffeted by pedestrians and reeling away from their affronted snorts of "I say, look here!"

Shielding my eyes against the glare, I strained to make out any signs of pursuit. As I had guessed, the carriage was hemmed in by horses and could not possibly turn about in time to catch me. Through the door I could just make out the hulking form of Brother Vinegar Tom within the shadowy cab, before a Hansom passed between us and blocked my view. Gambling that he would dare neither to doff his disguise, nor to be seen bull-masked in public, I staggered further away, glancing off the flanks of a passing horse, which shied and half-reared. The rider kicked out at me angrily but I was already gone.

When next I spotted the coach through the bustle, the door had been closed and it was pulling away from me. Of course, it had no identifying markings at all, being indistinguishable from any other medium-distance carriage. Straining my eyes, I managed to catch a glimpse of the driver before he rounded the corner, but even his identity was concealed by his long coat, upturned collar and winter hat.

My heart beat wildly in my chest and I glanced about to get my bearings, realising with a start that I was standing in London's Trafalgar Square after a recent light snowfall, and judged the time of day to be about noon.

I brushed away some snow from a wooden slat bench and, for a few moments, could do nothing more than sit still, breathe clean, cold air, and savour the simple miracle that found me still alive. For the first time in many months - in years, counting my service to Queen and Country - I was the captain of my own destiny.

The chill eventually roused me from this reverie and I began to seriously consider my options. First and most pressingly, I required money for food, warmth and board, and to procure a proper disguise, or a secure hiding place. Although I was free of Newgate Gaol and of the mysterious Hellfire Club, and I was, as far as anyone else in England was concerned, a dead man, it still would not do for me to be recognised by any passers-by, let alone by a Peeler. I was now plainly dressed, beardless and moustachioed, and I supposed that would have to be good enough disguise for the time being.

I rose and strode briskly against the cold wind, my mind racing. I must have money, but how? I could not conceive of how to find employment without attracting untoward attention, and would not beg, for to do so would be to risk the poorhouse. As sure as I was that the Hellfire Club would soon be searching for me, the local doss-houses and mendicants' quarters would be the best places to look.

I hazarded that ten hours had been spent in the darkened carriage, so my interview with the Club must have taken place around midnight, but I had no way of telling when, nor how, Brother Vinegar Tom might commence his own search. I hastened my step at this thought, wending my way through the crowds of Trafalgar Square and exiting into a quieter side-street.

I seemed to have been left with theft or robbery as my only choices and I was surprised to realise that I could not truly despise either course of action. As my rescuers and would-be captors of the Hellfire Club had impressed upon me, I was now a man with no name, thus free to take any name, or names. I felt unbound by the restrictions of family, friends and creed. In all honesty, though I had fought in no small array of battles prior to that time, I do not think that I had ever been quite so dangerous as at that moment. Like a fox, beset by hounds on all sides, I was ready to do anything to ensure my own survival.

I commenced to wander the streets of London Town, taking great care to avoid those areas that had suffered in the cholera epidemics of the previous year, and increasingly sure that Vinegar Tom, or some other cats-paw of the Hellfire Club, must already be on my trail.

After an hour or so I happened upon a battered old pair of spectacles in the gutter and snatched them up, straightening the wire as best I could with numbing hands; the lenses were badly scratched and it was still a poor excuse for a disguise, but every little helped.

As dusk settled, my mind turned inexorably to still darker thoughts and I began to feel very hungry. I pulled my scarf and jacket tighter about myself and walked down Shaftesbury Avenue towards Soho.
Men of well-to-do families bustled by, leading their wives, children and the children's nannies in brisk procession. At the corner, a "bottler" for a Punch and Judy show was assembling his audience. A cheery vendor offered passers-by their choice of roasted chestnuts and sweetmeats, and joked cheekily with a little girl playing with a bright green paper fan. Upon the surface, the scene was pleasant, colourful and industrious; a Bangalore street market in the heart of London town.

I looked deeper. Here were the urchins, sizing up their marks as the crowd gathered to watch the puppet show, *au fait* with every trick of the pickpocket's trade. Mr. Punch himself appeared upon the miniature stage, swazzling "Here we are again!", and then up popped the Devil, who led Punch a merry chase. I wondered idly whether the Punch and Judy professor was in with the young thieves.

Across the street, barely visible in the fading light, stood a small knot of men crowded around a folding table, upon which a fast-talker was shuffling three small cups – perhaps the second-oldest game. Just up ahead was stationed his lookout, scanning for Peelers. Ah, and here were young mistresses of the first-oldest game, a pair of painted girls under the watchful eye of their pander, a burly ruffian making a token effort to dress above his station.

The street-life of London revealed itself to me as I strode down Shaftesbury Avenue with my aching fingers and bandaged throat, hungry and utterly alone. Visions of Deviltry in a chaotic waltz with innocence and fun. The frigid wind picked up, fanning me with the scents of rich food from the pedlars' trays and from a small restaurant further down the street. At this my stomach cramped and my mouth watered with hunger pangs and I found myself scanning the side-streets for open windows through which I might unobtrusively squeeze, there to steal food or money, or both. Perhaps the "natural" morality of the moneyed gentleman was merely another luxury, when all else was said and done.

"That's the way to do it!" shrieked the hook-nosed Mr. Punch.

I was, just then, overcome by a strange sort of claustrophobia, and I turned abruptly up the gas-lit boulevard of Wardour Street, seeking distance from the crowds.

It began to snow more heavily and I hunched down, blowing flakes away from my lips. Perhaps ten paces along I was propositioned by a dollymop; "Out for a good time, lovey?" She was young and tolerably pretty, but I was in no mood for drabbing and of course had no money in any case, so I shook my head gruffly, pushing past her. The strumpet kept pace with me and then overtook, planting herself with hands on hips and blocking my way, her skirts swirling in the breeze.

"Oh come now, Sir; you have the look about you and no mistake on that score. You'll find no better in Soho, and that's God's honest truth."

I moved to push past again when suddenly a wiry arm wrapped about my neck from behind and I was hauled backwards into a shadowed alcove. The spectacles flew from my face. Choking and fearful of further damage to my throat, I gripped the arm with both hands but my injured fingers could exert no proper leverage. The man behind me was strong and there was a peculiar knack in his hold, a wrestler's trick of pressing against the base of my skull with one forearm. I was bent backwards and quite helpless.

The strumpet quickly glanced about her and then followed us in to the shadows, rifling through my pockets. Finding nothing, she swiftly unlaced and removed my boots, whispering "You just stay quiet, fine Sir, and we'll not be troubling you again."

Her accomplice squeezed tighter and I felt the pulsing accumulation of blood in my face. My vision began to dim and it seemed to me of a sudden that I was back on the Newgate scaffold. In that instant, seemingly of their own accord, my newly-bare feet shot up and out, driving into the woman's shoulder and flank and flinging her into the wall. At this, the garroter slung me down hard to the cobblestones and aimed a wicked stamping kick at my face. I writhed away and his heavy boot struck the paving. Cursing vilely, the woman dragged him back and they fled.

My first impulse was to find a constable, but of course that option was no longer available to me. I must maintain anonymity at all costs, yet the scoundrels had made off with my boots and they would not get away with them. I gathered myself together, shaking off the effects of the cowardly strangler's grip and searching for my spectacles. I could not find them in the shadows and so quickly wrapped my scarf over the lower part of my face as a makeshift disguise.

I rushed to the opening of the alcove, just in time to see movement in a patch of shrubbery a little further up and across the street. Scanning about for a weapon and finding nothing, I made towards that spot, snow soaking my stockinged feet, with no clear plan but to get back what was mine.

In a trice, I found myself on the other side and kneeling next to a smooth granite headstone, dusted with snow. The villains' footprints led into a graveyard.

The bushes grew on both sides of a high wrought-iron fence, and as I crouched down and began to push into them, I saw that some of the lower bars of the fence had been sawn away, leaving a concealed hatchway large enough for a man to crawl through. This was obviously a well-used bolt-hole, for other than the bushes masking the gap in the fence, there was easy passage and I wriggled through almost soundlessly.

In the murky moonlight I could make out a disorderly pattern of overgrown, seemingly untended graves and, a little distance away, a sturdy stone crypt. Tall weeds grew everywhere, save for a pathway where they had been pressed down. Calculating the lead the thieves had on me and moving with stealth, I followed their footprints; they had gone to ground on the other side of the mausoleum. As I drew closer, I could hear whispering.

"Why the devil did you pull me away, Tildy? I 'ad the bugger dead to rights!"

"Too much fight in that one. Decent boots, though. What's the evening's count?" The woman sounded nervous.

"Gawd, near enough three pounds, it looks like, and change besides!"

Again, I cast about for a weapon but could find not even a stout stick.

"Well, pass me my share and let's be done here. That last mark'll have the Peelers along any moment."

"All the more reason why we should 'ave finished 'im off."

"What, and 'ave the law down on us for murder? 'Urry up with that, Bill, you know I don't fancy this spot."

I noticed that one tall tombstone backed up almost against the wall of the crypt and a plan sprang to mind. Even weaponless, I could still make the best use of surprise. I boosted up on top of the stone and from that vantage had no great difficulty in climbing to the marble tile roof, though it was slick with moss and snow and my feet were growing numb. I kept crouched over, edging my way towards their voices.

Peering down, I saw that I was almost directly above the two of them. The villains were squatting on one of the steps, completely hidden from the street and sheltered from the snowfall, divvying up the cash from their evening's labours. The woman had my boots hanging around her neck by the laces.

I took a moment to judge the distance and then leapt down between them, my right forearm clubbing the man across the back of his neck, with much of my falling weight behind the blow. I hit him hard enough to stun my arm from elbow to wrist, though my still-tender fingers twinged sharply. The ruffian pitched forward as if pole-axed and lay still without so much as a grunt.

Landing upon practically nerveless feet, I stumbled down with him, but instantly pushed myself up off his back and spun about to face the woman – Tildy, he had called her. The painted trollop shrieked so as to wake the neighbouring dead from their rest and scrambled backwards up the steps in a panic, tripping and sprawling. I sprang at her and she cowered away, babbling "No Sir, please, 'e made me do it, I swear, I swear to you!"

I snatched a handful of her hair and thrust my face towards hers so close that we could have kissed, save for the scarf concealing my face. "Give me what is mine!" I hissed, and she fumbled my boots from around her neck, still whimpering apologies to me and recriminations against her erstwhile partner in crime. "If I ever see you again, I shall kill you," I rasped, and with that I thrust her away down the steps. She ran as if the Devil himself were at her heels, skirts flapping, in the direction of the hatchway.

I quickly stripped off my sodden socks, dried my feet as best as I could - which was not well - and hauled on the boots, praying that it was not too late to avert frost-bite. Then turned back towards Strangler Bill, who seemed to have been knocked completely senseless and lay stretched out upon his stomach.

This was my first chance to take a good look at the fellow – he was shorter and stockier than I, dressed in shabby layers of grey and brown wool. His felt cap lay some distance away. Against the chance that he was shamming, I approached from behind, wary of a sudden kick, but he showed no sign of life. Indeed, for a moment I wondered if I might have broken his neck but as I rolled him over it was clear that he was still breathing.

Notes and coins were scattered about him and I retrieved them as well as I could in the gloom. On a whim, I went through his pockets and found another wallet, evidently the spoils of a previous "job" that he had intended to keep for himself, and this I took as further payment for my troubles. It contained two pounds or so, bringing the total to nearly ten - a very solid sum!

I paused then and surveyed the scene. The graveyard had evidently been abandoned for some decades past. A number of the tombstones had fallen, and there were signs of vandalism and more than a few drinking sprees on this side of the crypt, with gin bottles scattered about. One of them might have made a fair substitute for a cosh, but that was by the way now. On three sides, the yard was backed by the windowless hulks of tall buildings; this was a shunned and largely forgotten spot.

As I made my way from the cemetery, the thought occurred to me that the would-be garroter might die of the cold if he did not regain his senses in good time. I kept walking. If there was any wrong in stealing from thieves, cheating cheats or profiting from the downfall of villains, then that was well beyond my present moral compass. I cared not a whit for his well-being.

I marched briskly back down Wardour Street, feet tingling as the blood returned to them and, with new-found confidence, re-entered the crowds streaming down the Avenue. The juggler's audience applauded and I tossed a penny into his hat. By this time, the snowfall was heavy enough that I would draw no undue attention by keeping the scarf wound about my face.

As Brother Farmara and Abbot Holt had impressed upon me, Jack Ashton was disgraced, executed and buried; all claims and titles void. Justice had not been done, but had been seen to be done; all was seeming sham and theatre.

Dead and then reborn, I had become a man with everything to gain. "*Fay ce que voudras*," indeed.

Beneath my mask, I began to grin.

Chapter 8

I stopped off at a modest but clean and, most importantly, warm dining room near Drury Lane. From the explosive *bonhomie* and *bon mots* resounding about the room, I took this to be a place where *literati* and theatre folk gathered. I found an out-of-the way booth and ordered a hearty poultry stew with buttered bread, roasted potatoes and a large mug of good dark beer, then set about surreptitiously laying out my socks upon the bench to dry and rubbing some more life back into my feet, doing my best not to wince at their prickling.

My thoughts turned again to my cousin Roland, who was at that very moment, presumably, enjoying the opulence of Ashton Hall.

Mindful of my scaffold-vow and encouraged by recent successes, not to mention well-fed and at least temporarily in funds, I could see no better moment to begin to plot my vengeance. Roland was now a wealthy and powerful man, and he had always been cunning; I would require time, planning and resources to enact a suitable revenge upon him.

In the short term, my most pressing concern was still to get some money; my profits of that evening's escapade would not last long, no matter how frugally I lived. It occurred to me of a sudden that the best and most appropriate source of income would be that which was rightfully mine in any case – the rents gathered from the various farms upon my estates in Surrey.

As I sipped my beer, my mission was revealed to me with crystal clarity; I would make my way incognito to Surrey, there to harass dear Roland's rent-collectors and steal back as good a portion of what was mine as necessary to fund my vendetta.

Thus resolved to the lately-unfashionable but undoubtedly rakish life of what the penny dreadfuls call a "Gentleman of the Road", I had but need of a suitable disguise…

Glancing distractedly about the room, I noticed one of the play-bills plastered upon the opposite wall;

The GRECIAN THEATRE
(Mr. B.O. Conquest, Sole Proprietor)
presents for the entertainment of all
MR. GEORGE CONQUEST
Late of the Drury Lane Theatre, the Albion, etc.
CELEBRATED ACTOR, ACROBAT and PANTOMIMIST
Performing as
MEPHISTOPHELES
In an elaborate production of
DR. FAUSTUS
Or
A DEAL With The DEVIL!
On Monday and during the week (Wednesday and Thursday excepted)

The bill was profusely, if rather crudely, illustrated; here was Mephistopheles himself, clad in tight-fitting scarlet, leaping from the very mouldings of the proscenium; there the Doctor cowered; here the demon struck a sinister pose, squatting frog-like atop a high mantel.

Now here was inspiration Devil-sent! If George Conquest could caper about the stages of London, in demon's guise no less, and profit therefrom, then I could surely do the same in my quest for revenge. In a fit of Mephistophelian inspiration, I finished my meal and, using the name "Jack Faust", booked into a nearby hostel for the night. As exhausted as I was, I took great satisfaction in being able to bolt my own door, from the inside.

Chapter 9

The next day I awoke to find my feet in tolerably good condition, bruises fading and showing no signs of damage from the cold. Likewise, by some miracle I had managed to avoid doing any further injury to my hands, which still seemed to be mending nicely. I booked out of the hostel and spent the remainder of that morning scheming and making some select purchases.

From a theatrical *costumier* I purchased a dark cloak and a fine devil's mask in scarlet Venetian leather, of which I felt sure that my Hellfire Club "patrons" would approve, as well as sundry hats, spectacles and other items of disguise. I spent some little time examining a false beard before deciding that, although it would undoubtedly be convincing enough when viewed across the footlights, it would not pass muster at close quarters and in the unforgiving light of day.

Some way away I came across a gun-smithy and outfitted myself with a serviceable pistol, a pocket holster and a brace of ammunition. Thus equipped, I repaired to the British Library, located and then quite without compunction stole a current map of the lands all about Ashton Hall, to study the most likely routes of the rent-collector's coaches.

In the afternoon, after having done what I could to alter my appearance, I strolled down Cecil Lane and into Charing Cross Road, which had always been one of my favourite London haunts, and popped in to a book vendor's. I had a mind to discover what I could of the Hellfire Club, its public history, at least. I was directed to a pamphlet titled "The Mad Monks of Medmenham", which seemed promising. Repairing to a nearby public house, I ordered a rum toddy and commenced to plan in earnest.

The first order of business was to enumerate my enemies and assess my present state of risk. Roland, obviously, presented no danger so long as he believed me to be safely dead. Now well-disguised, I judged the chances of my being recognised by a random passer-by, or by a constable on the streets, to be very slim.

The masked members of the Hellfire Club were wild cards in the deck; I could not, in all honesty, account them as "enemies" per se, for they had gone to such extraordinary lengths to save my life. However, it was quite obvious that, to them, I was merely a pawn in their "invisible war". Brother Farmara had mentioned that my health and well-being were important and that they had planned to keep me for some weeks or months, though for the life of me I could not fathom their motives.

Whilst I did not doubt that the Club had the resources and the will to track me down, neither did I believe that they would alert the police to assist them. They seemed far too secretive and self-contained for that sort of ploy. Also, I strongly suspected that many of their own activities were of an extra-legal nature.

My conclusion was that although the Hellfire Club might well try to re-capture me, they would take pains not to do me any serious harm. For my part, I had no serious compunctions about using my pistol to defend my freedom, if it came to that. I resolved to continue to change identities and guises, never resting too long in any one location, and to gather such intelligence about them as might give me the upper hand when it came to the pinch.

With that thought in mind and having checked that I had unimpeded access to the back door of the café, I started to read through the "Mad Monks" pamphlet.

Evidently, the name of the "Hellfire Club" had been used by a number of different fraternities throughout the last century. Most were devoted to Bacchus and Venus in equal parts, with sidelines in philosophical dilettantism, self-conscious blasphemy and raucous mischief. Members had been traditionally been very wealthy young rakes in the process of sowing their wild oats – notables of Dashwood's clique had included Robert Vansittart, William Hogarth and Francis Duffield. Much was made of Dashwood's service as a secret agent in the service of the Jacobites and his involvement with various Masonic sects in Italy.

Most intriguing were references to one of the latter-day Clubs' headquarters, in the catacombs beneath Medmenham Abbey on the Thames, near Marlow. I made a mental note to investigate those passages, should time and circumstance permit.

The next afternoon I was preparing to depart London for Surrey by the next available coach, having decided against rail travel both to save funds and towards keeping a low profile, when calamity struck.

I had paid my bill of fare at the proprietor's booth and was about to board when I was astonished to hear myself hailed by the coachman himself, up on the box seat.

"Cap'n Ashton, Sir!?"

Chapter 10

Of all the confounded luck, to be recognised now! I pretended not to hear the man and quickly boarded the coach, carrying my satchel with me. I was the last to enter and soon we were on our way, the journey to Guildford estimated to take twelve hours, depending upon the condition of the road.

Inside the cab we made our introductions and I discovered that I was travelling with a young couple of newly-weds from Leeds who were visiting the husband's mother's grave at Kingston Cemetery, not far from Ashton Hall, as it happened. I introduced myself briefly as Jack Dashwood and pleaded laryngitis to excuse myself from any further conversation. In truth, my voice was not yet fully recovered, but more importantly I had to consider the implications of the coachman having seen through my disguise. I had been counting against being spotted by anyone who had known Jack Ashton. After several years abroad I had filled out considerably, and I had never worn a moustache nor spectacles before. Curse the man's eyes, whoever he was!

I schemed rapidly, oblivious to the chatter of my travelling companions. He had called me Captain and Sir, so either he was an India hand, had known me during my training at Aldershot Camp, or conceivably had been one of the men I had met at Newgate. The latter seemed unlikely as my military background had not been a subject of discussion there, to my knowledge.

I could not place his voice and had not dared so much as a glance up in his direction before boarding. How much did he know? Surely notice of my trial and "execution" could not have escaped his attention – I knew that it had all been widely reported, making great press. I shook my head in mute frustration, as there was no way to answer the question of the man's identity and therefore no profit in wondering, for the time being. The fact was that he knew me and could expose me, whether deliberately or not, at any moment.

I knew that we would be stopping overnight at a coaching inn some distance to the South, and wildly wondered if I might choose the right moment and simply leap from the carriage. Such behaviour would doubtless alarm my fellow passengers yet would buy me some time to escape ... but to where? And surely, this would leave the coachman with enormous power over me, to alert the Peelers at the first opportunity, with clear knowledge of both my name and general whereabouts. No, I would have to ride this out and face the man at the next stop. Perhaps he could be bought.

The devil in me spoke ... "Perhaps he could be killed."

The remainder of the trip was passed in an agony of apprehension on my part, and much concern from my fellow passengers for "poor Mr. Dashwood" who was evidently feeling under the weather. The dear young woman sitting opposite me - Sarah McKenzie was her name - kept offering me sweet drinks and other little comforts, whilst her new husband tried to cheer me up by pointing out landmarks of note. The afternoon drew inexorably towards dusk and the coach drew ever closer to our rest-stop. I was sweating freely as we finally pulled in to the yard of a humble but pleasant-looking inn at Tandridge.

The McKenzies disembarked and I waited until they had made their way into the inn before following. The coachman was unloading their luggage from the rack, his back to me.

"Can I help you there, fellow?" I asked, sounding, absurdly, more chipper than I had in a fair while, while fingering the pistol in my pocket-holster. The coachman turned towards me and I almost staggered; it was none other than my old cavalry master from Aldershot, Ned Burrage!

"Pr'aps we can 'elp each other, Cap'n," he said quietly, his expression all but unreadable. "Check in now, and I'll meet you in the coachman's quarters in 'alf an hour's time."

Seemingly moments later, having assured the ever-concerned Sarah and her husband that I was indeed well enough to take a constitutional stroll, I was knocking upon his door, still stunned at the workings of fate. Sergeant Burrage had taken me under his wing when I was a young cadet, improving my riding and fencing, teaching me all the skills that had secured my survival as a captain with the Queen's Lancers in Bangalore. I could scarcely conceive as to how Fortune had conspired to re-unite us after all these years.

He ushered me inside, taking a moment to peer about the yard before closing and bolting the door and motioning for me to sit down. The room was close but comfortable and I chose one of two chairs by the fire.

"Ye're lookin' a little peaky, Cap'n," he said. "I've some rum here, would you care for a glass?"

"Thank you, yes."

He poured two and sat down in the chair opposite.

"Now Sir, if I may be so bold, just what the Devil is this all about? Last I 'eard, you was 'anging from a noose at Newgate. There was a picture in the broadsheet and all."

I paused to regard the old Sergeant. The Burrage who had been my instructor in the cavalryman's trade was a shrewd and very capable man, honest in his way, which was to say that he was profoundly honourable in large matters and possessed a healthy sense of proportion when it came to details. I had borne witness for him once, when he had been accused of thieving from the quartermaster; the false charge had been withdrawn upon my word.

I decided that I had little choice but to trust him with my tale, and so began, my voice lubricated with frequent sips of rum. I omitted some of the minutiae regarding the Hellfire Club, referring only to having been rescued by a gentlemen's fraternity with a flair for the dramatic. The telling took quite some time, and Ned sat largely silent throughout, puffing on a pipe.

"So that brings you up to date, Sergeant. My life and liberty are now in your hands."

"Hmm. I recall that once those roles were reversed, and ye did well by me, but all of this hinges on the charge of treason. It would be more than my life and debt to ye, to aid in the escape of a traitor from Her Majesty's justice."

"I've only my word, Ned - there's no proof until I find it."

"Then it comes down to the lad I knew as Jack Ashton and the man I see sitting before me now." Burrage set down his pipe, leaned forward in his chair and looked me straight in the eyes. I could do nothing but meet his gaze and hope for the best.

"The laddie I trained was a fine cavalryman and I 'eard that 'e did 'is country proud in India. 'e loved 'is father and did right by me when the moment came." He took a deep breath. "There are gentlemen and then there are gentlemen. I believe you, son."

He stood and offered his right hand, and we shook upon it. I have never felt quite so relieved, humbled, nor grateful as at that moment, and even now, so very many years later, I am not ashamed to say that its recollection brings a tear to my eye.

Ned then poured two more glasses and told me briefly of how he had come to be working as a coachman. A year after I had graduated from Aldershot and departed England, Ned had retired but found the quiet life of a widowed pensioner a tad too tame for his liking. At fifty-three he was still a robust and active man, accustomed to hard physical exercise and to the company of others of like mind. For a time he had taken to gambling on horses and the prize ring, which had rapidly depleted his savings; then he had come to a turning-point and decided to make something better of his life.

Ned's greatest ambition had always been to travel throughout England, and so when the opportunity had arisen, he had invested the remainder of his money into the carriage and a team of good horses. Few men could run a team like Ned Burrage, and although his income after taxes, tolls, stable rent and so-forth barely kept him solvent, he was popular with passengers and coachmen alike throughout the South, answered to no-one, and much enjoyed the life.

"So there is my story, Cap'n – not so colourful as yours, and that's a fact. The question is, what to do now? Of course, it will be my pleasure to transport ye safe to Surrey, but I wonder if we can't do better than that."

"I don't follow you, Ned."

"It's this, Cap'n – a powerful wrong has been done ye. I don't know many men who could have weathered that storm and come up smiling. It occurs to me that I might be of some use to ye in all of this. I 'ave friends all through London and right down to Sussex – inn-keepers, stablemen, butlers and the like. Some ex-Army. Good men, most of 'em, and the others 'ave their own talents." Ned paused to re-light his pipe.

"That, and the honest truth that this 'ighwayman lark of yours sounds like a right jolly time, and in a good cause, too. It 'minds me of me grand-da's tales o' the Scarecrow of Romney Marsh."

"As I recall, Ned, the Scarecrow was a masked marauder, a smuggler …"

"Aye, and so he was, but in a good cause, so me grand-da said. He protected the honest poor of the marshlands against King George's revenue men and fought the press gangs. And grand-da knew what he was about, Cap'n., for he was one of the Scarecrow's night riders, sure as I sit here …"

Ned seemed lost in reverie for a moment, but then barked out a laugh and slapped his thigh.

"Risky, o' course, very risky," he exclaimed. "Ye'll be needing 'orses and some spots to lie low " he grinned broadly through the fumes. "I'm yer man, Sir, if you'll 'ave me."

I was overwhelmed by the generosity of the old Sergeant's offer, having been steeling myself to undertaking everything alone. With tears in my eyes, I could only nod my assent.

"All right then. Get yerself back to yer room, before the passengers start to wonder too much, and I'll see ye bright and early. We'll say nothing more about this until we get to Guildford – should be tomorrow mid-day. Until then I'll bid ye a good night, Cap'n."

We shook hands again and I made my way back across the yard and entered the Inn. Fortunately, it had not snowed in the interim, and so I had no need to explain my dry clothes to Sarah and her husband, whose name I confess that I had forgotten in my distraction, but which turned out to be Alan. They insisted on treating me to a meal and had obviously been concerned for my well-being. I found their courtesy and compassion to be most touching, and felt badly for deceiving them. Privately, I swore that no such good folk as Ned and the McKenzies would ever suffer if I had any say in the matter.

Upon arrival at Guildford the next day, I bade the young couple a fond farewell and rode on with Ned to a small stable, a few miles out of the town, upon which he shared the lease. He told me that the co-lessor, one Edwin Hunt, would be pursuing business in the North for some months to come, so we had the place entirely to ourselves.

I helped him tend to the horses and then we sat down upon two hay bales to consider our next move. We agreed that he should use his local contacts to determine the dates of Roland's next rent collection and the routes his men would take. Meanwhile, I should keep a low profile, for in all of England, I was most likely to be recognised by the good people of Guildford and nearby Aldershot Camp, who might recall me as Sir Cecil Ashton's son. Likewise, the Hellfire Club, knowing full well that Surrey was my home and that I had cause to seek out Roland, might have agents there awaiting my arrival.

Ned went about his business and I remained sequestered in a small attic to the back of the stable loft, where we had arranged such basic accommodation as we could. Restless, I divided my time between exercise in the barn and the consideration of my plans. As if planning a military incursion, I pored over the map, pondering the best means of gaining my goals without resorting un-necessarily to violence: it was one thing to kill an enemy in times of war, but given time to reflect, I would prefer not to kill Englishmen if that could be avoided.

I considered methods of sure escape and the counter-tactics that I might reasonably anticipate from my enemies. Highway robbery being out of fashion for the best part of fifty years, the chances were good that I should have surprise firmly on my side, at least during the first escapade. Thereafter, affairs might become sticky.

I sorted through my satchel and lifted out the Devil mask. By the light of day, it seemed rather a tawdry, burlesque thing; yet I recalled the stunning success of my improvised tactics against the two thieves in the graveyard, the man knocked unconscious in an instant, and the woman almost superstitiously terrified …

After several days on the roads around Guildford, Ned had gathered the information that we required. As was common practice amongst unscrupulous land-owners, Roland had hiked up the rents and summarily evicted those families who were patently unable to meet his demands, some of whom had been farming the land for many generations. He had then recruited as his rent-collectors some of the worst men in the district, well paid bravos who also served as his bodyguards and bully-boys. In the space of a few months many of "his" remaining tenants had been reduced almost to penury, and some were desperately struggling.

Ned's sources also confirmed that Roland was currently resident at Ashton Hall, where he had become roundly despised by the staff. It was apparent that my cousin had very quickly established himself as a petty tyrant in Surrey.

"I 'ave cousins 'ere meself, Cap'n," Ned explained, "but 'ad not known the situation was so dire. Praise God, my kin are apothecaries in Guildford township, not tenant farmers, but even they 'ave dire stories of Sir Roland Ashton and 'is bravos. They say the man is mad."

"Perhaps, but he is not a fool. My cousin is the worst sort of foe, cunning and ruthless. Well, I shall be a thorn in his side."

It was Roland's practice to have his men return all their takings to the safe at Ashton Hall, where it was kept secure until the time came for transport to his bank in London. That transport, of course, would happen by rail-car.

"Roland's men will be making their next rounds two days hence," I mused. "It seems to me that the moment to strike will be while the strong-box is in transit between Ashton Hall and Guildford Station."

"Pardon me, Cap'n, but there would be less risk in taking what ye can from individual collectors. The coach carrying the strong-box is bound to be well-guarded, and no offence, Sir, but ye've never done this before."

"True enough, but any minor action on our part ahead of time would warn Roland of trouble. He'd take extra precautions and we might lose the main chance."

Ned eventually agreed to my plan (although I'm sure that I heard him mutter "young hot-head" at least once) and via the map we decided upon the best spot for my highwayman's *debut*. The collection round was to begin in two days, and would probably take another two days to complete. Allowing that the money would be held overnight and under heavy guard at Ashton Hall, that suggested the following Monday as the most likely date for transport to the Station. We had plenty of time to prepare.

Ned went in to the town that night, and returned with intelligence that confirmed Roland's schedule. The passage of his money-coach through Guildford was a regular event, which seemed incautious of my cousin. I briefly wondered if it was some form of ruse, or if he had simply grown ostentatious and complacent. That chance I would have to take.

The next day I borrowed one of Ned's horses and, dressed as a surveyor so as not to attract any undue attention, scouted the chosen area carefully. It was a point where the road from Ashton Hall took a fork, one branch leading to nearby Guildford, and the other out into open heath-land before crossing a bridge over the River Wey. Right beside the road and some dozens of yards back from the fork there rose a small half-hillock, perhaps fifteen feet in height; the road curved somewhat around it. My purloined map named this spot as Milton's Fork.

For the remainder of the week I made frequent journeys between the barn and the site, sending Ned into town for certain provisions as required. I rehearsed as well as I was able, and then had nothing to do but wait ...

Chapter 11

HIGHWAY ROBBERY

My keenest recollection of this, my first escapade as a highwayman, is of a terrific confusion of scarlet smoke and sparks.

It was late in the afternoon when, from my lookout point atop the hillock, I spotted Roland's men making their way slowly along the road to Guildford, bound for the evening train to London. As we had surmised, the coach was well-guarded indeed. Aside from the driver, there was a man some way to the front, riding a piebald horse and evidently serving as point; two men riding dark horses to either side of the coach itself, occasionally falling back or pressing on a little, and a fourth man bringing up the rear. Even from this distance and in the fading light, I could tell that all but the driver were armed with long guns.

As they drew closer I could make out more detail. The fellow in front evidently took his job seriously, and scanned his gaze about warily. I lit a cigar, careful to conceal the spark of the match, and waited. A few minutes more, and I lost sight of him as he passed beneath my vantage, the coach and other riders following some twenty yards behind. I had counted on the procession being closer together, but there was nothing for that now. I checked my supplies and prepared to act.

Ghost, Devil or Highwayman?

Has "Spring Heeled Jack" Returned to Haunt the South?

A terrible encounter, almost without parallel in England, has taken place near Guildford, Surrey, between five men in the employ of Sir Roland Ashton and a bold thief styling himself as a "Spring Heeled Jack". The particulars to hand are but meagre, owing to the intelligence having only been received at our London office yesterday evening, but they are of such a character as to show that a most unscrupulous and extraordinary criminal is at large in the

South, and that no effort must be spared to secure him immediately. As will be seen from the following telegram, received last night from our Surrey correspondent, two men have been injured, a third nearly drowned, while the fate of Mr. Lanigan is dubious:—

"GUILDFORD, Monday, 9 P.M.

"News has just reached Guildford that Messrs. Reynolds, Collopy, Lanigan, Smith and Fitzpatrick, all employed as rent collectors in the service of the honourable Sir Roland Ashton of Ashton Hall, have been attacked and robbed by a lone highwayman at Milton's Fork, about 5 miles from here. Constable McIntyre is currently searching the site of the attack and has deputised other men to scour the surrounding area."

The offender referred to by our correspondent is said to have emerged from a cloud of smoke and stinging red sparks, by means of a tremendous leap that carried him to the roof of the coach driven by Mr. Lanigan. This coach was transporting a sum of Sir Roland's money for transit to London by rail-carriage. In the confusion, the horses ridden by Messrs. Smith and Collopy panicked and bolted for some distance before they could be calmed, by which time the robber had apparently thrown Mr. Lanigan from the driver's seat and was making off with coach and team together. Mr. Fitzpatrick, who had been guarding the coach from the rear, had the best view of what had transpired and his testimony is as follows;

"I was following behind the coach as usual when suddenly all ____ broke loose up ahead. At first I reckoned the coach was afire for there was smoke and showers of sparks everywhere and that was when Jem and Andy's (Messrs. Collopy and Smith, respectively – Ed.) horses broke and ran. I saw the brigand clearly, he flew right through the air and landed on top of the coach like a great bat. He was a terrible sight, he had a bright red face and was wearing all black, with a cape or wings that flapped. He appeared out of no-where, he did.
Then of a sudden I heard Lanigan cry out; he went falling down off the seat and the coach took off. I tried to give chase but the smoke was billowing out and my horse couldn't see no more than I could. We nearly ran into a stile down the road and he threw me into the snow. That's all I remember."

Mr. Lanigan appears to have fled the scene shortly thereafter and has not re-appeared. Constable McIntyre, together with the man's family in Guildford, are appealing for any information as to his whereabouts.

Mr. Collopy, Mr. Smith and Mr. Reynolds, the latter of whom had been riding some distance ahead, gave chase as the coach was driven away from Guildford at reckless speed. Being hampered by the smoke and encroaching darkness, none of these men were able to describe the highwayman in any detail, but Mr. Reynolds, who had glimpsed him as he wheeled his horse about, said that the villain appeared to be wearing a black cloak and agreed with Mr. Fitzpatrick that his face had seemed bright red in colour. "Like the very Devil," he said. Mr. Reynolds fired several times towards the outlaw, but could not see well enough to take proper aim. "If I did hit him, it did no good," Mr. Reynolds said.

Shortly thereafter the coach crossed a narrow bridge over the River Wey and the valiant pursuers made to follow, but were nonplussed when the centre of the bridge collapsed in a fiery blast mere moments after the coach had crossed. Mr. Reynold's horse, which was in the lead of the pursuers, reared at this event and could advance no further and the horses of Messrs. Smith and Collopy, coming up close behind, threw their riders, the former landing upon the bridge and the latter in the river. As Mr. Collopy could not swim, his colleagues had to go to his aid and were unable to mount any further chase.

Two of the men recall the "uncanny, shrieking laughter" of the spring-heeled robber as the coach sped away in the direction of Woking Village. It was found later that evening, the horses grazing quietly in a paddock some distance outside Woking, denuded of the strongbox that had contained some three hundred and fifty pounds.

Representatives for the honourable Sir Roland Ashton said that their master was deeply annoyed by this outrage and would immediately begin his own investigation into the affair.

The alert reader may well wonder at several details of this report, which was both surprisingly accurate and entirely satisfactory to me at the time. Firstly, the scarlet smoke and sparks had been the product of a dozen clay-shell fireworks that I had made, with chemicals procured from faithful Ned's cousin Albert, who was an apothecary in Guildford, and gunpowder from the brace of bullets that I had purchased in London. Equipped with short fuses, lit with the glowing end of the cigar and lobbed down at the carriage and horsemen, their effect was spectacular. I had retained another dozen in a satchel slung about my back, whose use I shall explain presently.

My flying leap, described in such thrilling terms by the unfortunate Mr. Fitzpatrick, was easily the most hazardous and, if I may say, ingenious aspect of the caper. It was accomplished by means of a long ash-wood plank that I had hinged to two posts sunk into the top of the hill. While the men below were trying to reign in their panicked steeds, it was a simple matter to send one end of the plank toppling over the edge of the hillock. Thus it projected some ten feet out and a few feet above the top of the coach, albeit at a rather greater distance away than I had hoped. I had no time for second thoughts at that stage and so proceeded to run along the plank, cigar clenched between my teeth, and take a flying leap from the end of it, as if off a gymnast's spring-board.

I had the luck of the Devil throughout the entire caper, but never more than when I was flying through the air towards the roof of the coach, where I alighted, exulting, an instant later. The driver must have heard the thump for he turned towards me, saw a smoke-breathing demon staring back, screamed and flung himself out of his seat.

At this point I slung the satchel off my shoulder and lit one of the firework/bombs within, which ignited the others in turn, tossed the satchel onto the rails atop the carriage roof and then grasped the reigns and made hell-for-leather towards the bridge, streaming clouds of stygian smoke and crimson sparks behind.

The explosive collapse of the bridge (which, I regret to say, caused no small inconvenience to the local people until it was repaired) was engineered with black-powder charges beneath the boards, short fuses triggered by a light trip-wire as my horses charged across – the same scheme that I had been maliciously accused of plotting against Her Majesty's coach. In my surveyor's guise I had taken the precaution of erecting light barricades, easily trampled down by horses at full gallop, at both ends of the bridge, warning off any others who might have attempted to cross it before me. It was a near thing for all concerned but every detail of the plan had worked out in my favour and I could not contain the whoops of triumphant laughter as I made good my escape.

Meanwhile, as Fitzpatrick lay senseless, Lanigan was fleeing for his very soul and your narrator was leading the other three a merry chase, faithful Ned was back at the hillock, concealing my springboard and powdering any traces of the firework-bombs beneath his boots. He had a broad smile upon his face and stories of his grandda's night rider days firmly to mind. We met scarcely an hour later at the appointed spot, where he helped me load the strongbox into his coach, then left the carriage and horses safe and sound before taking a circuitous route back to the stables outside Guildford.

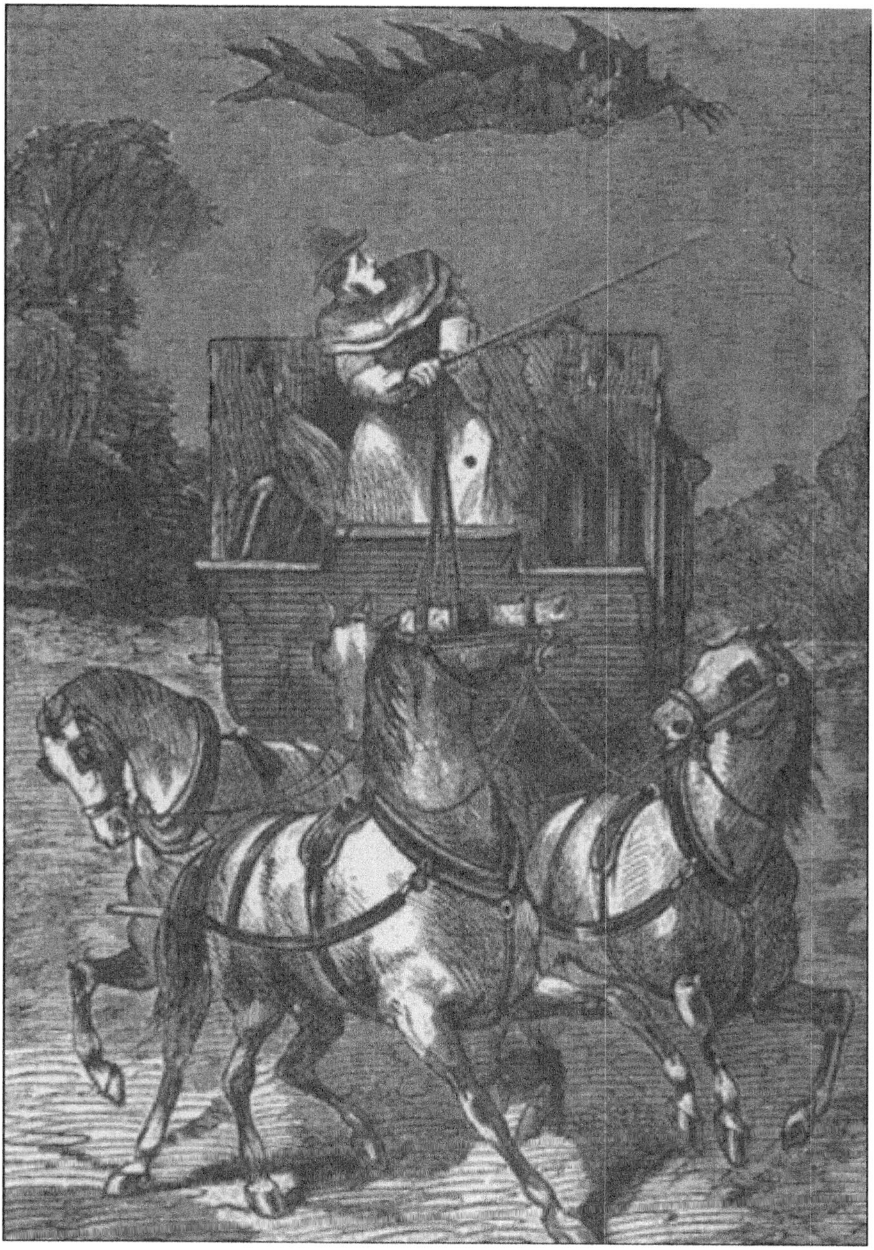

Chapter 12

It was two days later that Ned burst excitedly into my room, waving a newspaper and laughing with glee.

"Jack, me lad, yer famous! Look at what they're sayin' about ye!"

I read the report through and could not help but join the sergeant in his mirth.

"And it's all over Guildford!" he continued, gasping for breath and wiping tears from his eyes. "All over the country, I shouldn't wonder. 'Spring Heeled Jack', eh? Trust those newspaper men. D'ye recall the stories, Cap'n?"

I did indeed. The legend of the Spring Heeled Jack was well-known throughout England. He was held to be a demon or ghost and was renowned for his great leaps and terrifying appearance. Many were the men of my generation who had known the thrill of dread as children, when told by our nurses that "Springle Jack" would come for us in our sleep if we mis-behaved, and steal our breath away. "And it don't matter that you sleep up on the second floor, for he'll just jump in through your window. You can't get away from him, oh no! So you just mind your manners, Master So-and-so!"

There were also travellers' tales of men found dead upon the roadsides in lonely spots, their faces a rictus of fear but their bodies unmarked, the only evidence of the cause of their mortal fright being deep, cloven footprints driven into the earth all about.

In any case, Ned, who was positively chortling, continued that our escapade had some of the good folk of Guildford and the surrounding area re-assessing the character of Spring Heeled Jack. There was no great love lost for "Sir" Roland in these parts, and the sheer audacity and romance of the robbery had captured the popular imagination.

Opinion on the streets and in the public houses seemed divided on whether "Jack" was a mortal highwayman - a latter-day Dick Turpin - or a supernatural entity, perhaps, it was whispered, sent by Old Nick himself to destroy the bridge over the Wen, which would cause all manner of problems. The logic of the Devil sending one of his minions to rob an earthly villain escaped me, but I felt certain that the townspeople would come up with a reasonable explanation over their mugs of ale, that very night if not sooner.

Now this was an interesting development. By trading on the name bequeathed to me by the papers - and the lore behind it - perhaps I could strike fear into the hearts of some of those who stood between my fortune and myself. Roland himself was an educated man, far too worldly to be taken in by such superstition, but recalling the look on Mr. Lanigan's face and his short flight from the driver's seat, I could see a tactical advantage in the plan.

If the people of Surrey wanted Spring Heeled Jack in all his devilish glory, then I was resolved to play that part to the very hilt.

Well-funded – quite surprisingly so - and encouraged by our success, Ned and myself had several days of leisure to consider our course of action. For his part, the old Sergeant would keep up appearances by maintaining his coach routes through the South, while gathering such information as he could. His itinerary would have him away from Guildford for the next ten days. For mine, I had some ideas as to bringing "Jack" to life and was eager to get started on that project. I spent the rest of that day in a fever of invention, making sketches and jotting down a list of items for Ned to procure. For those that he could not find in Guildford, "Jack Hood" sent away money-orders to London.

On Sunday morning, we bade each other farewell. I was struck, as the coach pulled away, by how dear and trusted a friend he had become to me.

My first order of business that day was to set up a makeshift *ghendkhana*, an Indian-style gymnasium, in the barn. I had not taken proper exercise since I had left Bangalore, and needed to get back into peak condition for my new role.

I smoothed and then sunk a stout, tall fence pole deep into the soil towards the rear of the barn, there to serve as a *malla-khamb*, one of the principal pieces of equipment of the Hindoo wrestler and acrobat. My tutor in Bangalore, Guru Alli, had taught me only the basics of the art, as to master it, one must begin such training almost from infancy; yet it was an unsurpassed way to develop the sinews and overall strength and agility. The object was to treat the post as a combination of wrestling opponent and gymnastic partner, climbing and winding oneself about it in all manner of strenuous contortions.

This task took the best part of the morning. I resolved to spend no less than two hours per day cultivating my strength, nimbleness and wind, in anticipation of the physical challenges that were sure to lie ahead.

Next, and most intriguing, perhaps, was the matter of how to accomplish "Jack's" prodigious leaps. I could hardly prepare springboards all over the show, and so would require some other means of self-propulsion. One variant of his legend had him literally bounding along with springs in the soles of his boots, and I had sketched some tentative designs along these lines the day before. With a sense of mischief, I decided to construct the base or "sole" of each boot in the manner of a cloven hoof.

My initial experiments that afternoon involved an assembly of horseshoes and six of the new "bed-springs", which were intended to replace cotton batting in mattresses, affixed to the soles of my boots. My ankles barely survived my first attempt to run whilst thus encumbered, and the experiment was an utter failure. I devoted the remainder of the afternoon to general exercise, and retired early to bed that night.

Within the week, most of the other items we had ordered had arrived, and I spread all of "Jack's" potential equipment out on the workbench. I doubt that anyone coming across the assembly by chance could possibly have guessed the use to which they might, if I had the ingenuity and luck, be profitably put.

From a theatrical supply company, I had ordered a pair of knightly gauntlets, an elegant articulation of shining steel plates over soft leather padding, with palms of chain-mail. Each included a greave that covered my forearms almost up to the elbows.

From other *costumiers*, a tight-fitting cuirass of deep scarlet leather, with flared epaulettes; a workman's utility harness; a sturdy, wide belt with a large silver buckle, two black silk shirts, a pair of tall boots and a supple leather capelet.

From the neighbouring saddlery, assorted panels of tough, cured leather, padded with horsehair.

From the dental equipment supplier in London; canisters of compressed ether together with an assortment of valves, India rubber tubes and sealants.

From a photographic supply house; a large vial of liquid magnesium and a wad of cotton.

Finally, from Ned's cousin Albert in Guildford town, an array of chemicals; saltpetre, sodium nitrate, lampblack and various metallic salts and powders, together with a miscellany of pyrotechnical appliances.

Thus prepared, I spent the following few days in a state of continual experimentation, almost, I confess, bordering on the obsessive. When at last all was ready to my satisfaction, I turned my attention again to the problem of the spring-boots. In the midst of my other labours, the thought had struck me that I could do no better than to imitate that famous beast of the far Antipodes, which the natives call the "kanguru".

Recalling what I could of kanguru locomotion and physiology, I hazarded that their leaping prowess was due to their abnormally long and well-developed Achilles tendons. All very well for the kanguru, but how to apply this towards my present problem? I glanced about the barn distractedly, seeking inspiration ...

Three days later, I was overcome with a sense of euphoria as I sailed with room to spare over a pyramid of hay-bales stacked to the height of roughly six feet, my spring-heels developed to perfection!

My breakthrough had come when I realised that no contrivance of coil-springs affixed to the sole of a boot would ever afford me the agility that I sought. The key, as I had intuited, lay in the mechanical adaptation of kanguru locomotion, and my inspiration was discovered when I had noticed several long, slim carriage-springs hanging from a hook over the work bench.

I had spent that morning constructing two thin but sturdy steel platforms, patterned to match the soles of my boots. Each platform was stabilised by two struts, which ran up either side of my calves. Each strut, in turn, was firmly affixed to a padded leather brace that fit just under my knee. Descending down from behind the heel of each platform, rather in the manner of an acrobat's stilt, was a curved, eighteen-inch-long carriage spring, split wide at the base both to provide stability and to form the "cloven hoof" effect, wound about with thick India-rubber straps. The spring bars were fixed to a strong hinge system and could fold up against the back of my calves when not in use.

With the springs extended, I could strap my boots onto the platforms, secure my lower legs into the struts, and hence stand close to seven feet in height, balanced upon the hooves. Most importantly, the extraordinary tensile strength of the spring-steel served as an artificial Achilles tendon, greatly amplifying my running speed and the length and height of my leaps.

Ned arrived back at the stables that evening. Once he had tended to the horses he was quite obviously bursting with anticipation to see these mysterious devices put to use and I confess that I shared his excitement.

Firstly, I donned the harness, then the mask and spring-heeled boots, and finally the steel gauntlets, leaving aside some of the other items for safety's sake. Even partially equipped, I was starting to get the feel of my new role. We cleared a space about the size of a prize-fighting ring, bordered with hay bales. When all was ready I asked my companion to act the part of one of Roland's bravos, and tossed him a singlestick - a stout ash cudgel with a tough wicker-work handguard.

"Cap'n, yer sure of this?" he asked quietly, hefting the club in one hand.

"I'm not sure at all, good fellow; so better we should test today than rue tomorrow. Have at me, now!" and I playfully motioned as if to attack him. Ned responded with some alacrity – he had swung more than the occasional cudgel in his day – and jabbed at my chest. I swatted this aside with the back of my left gauntlet and sprang high to the right, landing some yards away, in a wrestler's crouch.

Warming to the sport, Ned advanced upon me, feinted a low jab, then swung a hard back-hander towards my left shoulder. I caught this easily with the grieve over my right forearm, and in the same movement managed to bring the edge of the other gauntlet down across the cudgel, cracking it in half. I felt not a thing of either blow.

"Tricks, eh?" Ned retrieved another weapon and began to attack in earnest, calling upon his training with the cavalry sabre. For my part, I resorted to treating the cudgel as if it were the gloved fist of a pugilist. The gauntlets and grieves painlessly parried every swing, thwarted every thrust. Once he landed a downright blow against the mask, and once a lucky thrust to the ribs; the padding that I had sewn into the leather absorbed these, and although I felt the impact, there was little pain and no injury.

Finally I managed to catch one of his swipes on the backswing with the palm of my gauntlet, and I was able to wrench the stick from his grasp. In his effort to retain the weapon he staggered forwards a little and at that I vaulted right over his head, bounced once and then alighted on top of the coach behind him. Thus disarmed he spun about, and for a moment, did not see me; then, glancing up, the old soldier grinned from ear to ear.

"Enough, Cap'n! I warrant that even if I came at ye with a sword, I should not so much as be able to touch ye. Well done indeed!"

I flexed my hands and thought it good enough practice for the moment.

"But what if there be more than one blackguard in need of a thrashing? Or what if ye 'ave need to stow one for a spell, without, if ye please, spiking him down with those iron gloves?"

"Ah, Ned, think back to your childhood. Do you not recall the magic of Spring Heeled Jack, that steals the breath away from naughty boys? The sulphurous smoke that heralds the arrival of the demon upon this mortal coil?"

At this he frowned somewhat.

"What 'zactly do ye have hid in that devil's get-up?"

"All shall be revealed, and soon, I hope." I doffed the mask, which was wet with sweat, and began to remove the harness, well-pleased with it. "Now, tell me – what news is there?"

Ned filled his pipe and we sat down on the hay-bales.

"First off, the Spring Heeled Jack is the talk of the South, and the other points of the map, I'd warrant," he began. "I met a fellow at Barlowe who was kin to one of the rent-men – Collopy, if I recollect aright – and he thought it fine sport that 'is nephew should 'ave ended up ducked in the Wen."

"And what of Lanigan, the driver?"
"He turned up in Guildford and swears 'e saw the Devil 'imself. Roland is in a high dander and has vowed to track ye down, I 'eard that from young Constable McIntyre's ma. No-one's seen hide nor hair of 'His Lordship' since the, er, since we helped him to collect yer rent, but the word about Guildford is that he is none too pleased with the newspapers, nor with the folk who are callin' Spring Heeled Jack a hero."

"A hero?"

"Aye, that's what some are sayin'."

"Good Lord!"

Some of the people of Guildford seemed to have cast me as Robin Hood against Roland's Sheriff of Nottingham. Of course, my motives were not so altruistic, but surely it did no harm to have the common folk on my side, and I took some pleasure in imagining Roland's reaction to all of this. I intended that my cousin should have received his comeuppance well before the next round of rent collections. What I needed now was an excuse to pit "Spring Heeled Jack" against him more directly, to show him up as the cowardly poltroon he truly was.

We passed the remainder of the evening in pleasant conversation until Ned, tired by his exertions on the road, retired to bed.

Chapter 13

A mere two days passed before Spring Heeled Jack was called into action again, under very different circumstances. I was chafing somewhat at being confined to the stables as it was, my daily routine having fallen into a pattern of exercise upon the post and swinging makeshift Indian clubs, making minor adjustments to my equipment, and practice with the boots. Late one afternoon, as I was springing about over an improvised obstacle course of hay-bales, Ned rode into the barn in a state of high consternation.

"Cap'n! Roland's men are in the town, and causing all manner of mischief!"

We quickly prepared another horse as Ned explained the situation. My cousin had apparently sent his bully-boys into Guildford to retrieve the unfortunate Mr. Lanigan, who had sent in his notice and was staying with his family. Evidently he was a rather simple fellow, a youth whose way with horses had found him employment with Roland's household, but who was otherwise blameless of the thuggery that characterised the new regime at Ashton Hall.

Roland had demanded to interview him regarding the robbery, suspecting that he was an accomplice, but Lanigan refused to leave his mother's house for fear of meeting Spring Heeled Jack upon the road, and so matters had come to a head.

As it stood, when Ned had come across the scene, Roland's men had reacted badly to their reception at the Lanigans' abode, the family being Irish and disinclined to allow their frightened boy to be carted off against his will, and a riot was brewing in the main street.

Now here was a fine chance to test my fettle and give Roland's nose another good tweaking into the bargain!

I snatched up those items of "Jack's" equipment that I was not already wearing and we rode hard for the town, shouting tactics back and forth. Ned was to hold back and assist in my escape if necessary; I would seek what high ground I could. We agreed to rendezvous back at the stables unless circumstance dictated that we follow our own fortunes.

As we approached Guildford I had no difficulty in perceiving the site of the trouble. A large crowd was gathered in High Street, shouting abuse at Roland's men who were, at the present moment, in a tense confrontation with the Lanigan clan and their neighbours. A young constable was attempting to keep order.

I veered my horse away from the scene and down a shadowy alley leading behind the row of shops and houses facing the street, reigning him in when we came to a courtyard sheltered by high fences on three sides. With the fervent hope that all eyes were upon the High Street, I slipped on my costume and what remained of the armory, then lifted the catches that held the springs in place along the back of my boots. The curved steel bars snapped into position and I bounced once, vaulted over the wall, from thence at a single bound across the courtyard and then up a staircase that led to a balcony on the second story.

As I sprang up to the rooftop, I could hear angry shouts and the sounds of scuffling from the street on the other side.

Quickly scanning the roof-scape I noticed a small bell-tower some way to my left, and without pausing to think, I bounded across to it, clearing chimney-pots and gables. A quick glance down into the High Street revealed that Roland's men had succeeded in dragging young Lanigan from his sanctuary. They were trying to load him into a cart, but were having a hard time of it fending off blows from the blackthorn shillelaghs wielded by his aggrieved uncles, aunts and cousins.

If it was news of the Spring Heeled Jack that Roland wanted, then that worthy would oblige him. I gripped the brass bell with both steel-shod gauntlets and heaved it back and forth, ringing for all that I was worth

"Spring Heeled Jack" and the Guildford Panic

Demon Takes to the Rooftops, Witnesses Report

An extremely fanciful broadsheet rendition of my encounter with Roland's men upon the rooftops of Guildford. For the record, there was no gunfire, nor did the good townspeople find it necessary to throw stones at me.

Our Surrey correspondent informs us of another visitation by the phantom assailant known as "Spring Heeled Jack", whose appearance has sparked a panic in the normally peaceful town of Guildford.

GUILDFORD, Wednesday, 7.00 p.m.

The Spring Heeled Jack first appeared in the bell tower overlooking High Street, ringing the bell and alerting a large number of townsfolk to his presence, and the street was soon filled with terrified witnesses to his uncanny leaping antics. Constable Ian McIntyre and a party of men in the employ of the Honourable Sir Roland Ashton raced up to the roofs through the nearest buildings to confront the menace but he evaded them by springing about.

The leaper himself was described by witnesses as being of devilish appearance, clad in close-fitting scarlet and black and towering some eight feet in height. He bore a capelet or pair of short wings that flapped as he sprang from archway to chimney-top with inhuman ease, quite outdistancing the valiant efforts of his pursuers as they scrambled about the dangerous heights.

One of the men, Mr. George Reynolds, who had lately encountered Spring Heeled Jack upon the road outside Guildford, was seen by many townspeople to grip the Demon by his cape at the very edge of the roof, at which moment his adversary wheeled about and appeared to vomit a silvery-blue vapour into his face. Mr. Reynolds then staggered back and nearly fell, bringing forth screams from many women in the crowd below.

Three other men in the party are reported to have finally brought the creature to bay upon a high balcony when they were dazzled by a flash of lightning, seemingly issued from the body of Spring Heeled Jack himself. This event, likewise, was noted by numerous witnesses who were straining to follow the rooftop chase from their vantage in the High Street.

The phantom was then seen to spring to the top of a gable, at which point the pursuers were frustrated in their efforts to follow him, due to the steep slope. A great quantity of scarlet mist or smoke then spread about the roof and ringing laughter was heard, throwing the pursuers into further confusion, the phantom thereby making good his escape.

Sir Roland Ashton's servants have been forbidden by their master to speak of this incident, but Mr. Reynolds, upon being awakened from his stupor and rescued from the roof, is reported by witnesses to have said;

"I had the fellow by his coat and was of a mind to sling him over the edge, but then he spun about and stared at me. He had the Devil's face, all creased and snarling, with horns upon his head. His eyes were aglow. He hissed at me like a cat and I smelled something sickly sweet, and that is all I remember. Next time I will be ready for his tricks, mark my word."

Constable McIntyre has been called to report directly to his superiors in London and this journey shall be made as soon as he has recovered from a twisted ankle and a minor concussion, the injuries being suffered when he fell back on to the roof in his attempt to scale the gable.

This caper had been one close call after another, and I had been quite exhilarated by the time I dropped down into the courtyard. I fled from the scene on horseback, having merely doffed mask and gauntlets in my haste to put distance between myself and the town, and met Ned upon the road. We made our way over open heath towards the stable, against the chance of pursuit, taking care not to come within eyeshot of Guildford; however, it seemed that we were well away by the time my erstwhile sparring partners realised that "Jack" was no longer amongst them.

Ned had watched what he could of the rooftop battle from across the street, and was abuzz with questions.

"Cap'n, how did ye contrive that great flash of light?"

"Magnesium, good fellow, like a photographer's flash-pan." I went on to explain that my harness included three shielded panels of black cotton, soaked in the chemical and backed with sturdy leather padding, which could be instantly fired by flicking a trigger built into the belt.

"Ingenious, Sir, I'll give ye that. But what under Heaven happened to that man who had ye by the cape? That were a near thing indeed. He collapsed, yet I did not see ye strike him."

"There was no need. I have built two tubes into the sides of my mask, leading to canisters of ether and chloroform worn in the back of my harness. They are quite hidden beneath the cloak. When the ruffian seized me I simply held my breath and switched a valve, and he got a good dose right in the face."

My companion was so impressed that I did not trouble to tell him, as I do you, now, that I had swooned myself the first time I had tested this particular apparatus, having over-estimated the power of the compressed gas to jet away from my own nose and mouth. Fortunately I was testing only a short burst, else the results might have been serious indeed. As it was, waking up, light-headed and silly, moments later in the dust of the stable floor, I had cursed myself for a fool and practiced the manoeuvre on farm animals until satisfied with it. Few memories of my experimentations are quite so strange as that of the sight of sheep and goats staggering drunkenly about the barn before keeling over in a state of euphoria.

Days later, once the newspaper had printed its report, the Spring Heeled Jack mania was well under way. Ned kept up a faithful diary and scrapbook of this period. For the time being, it will suffice to quote from a few letters to the editors of various papers, simply to give some indication of the public fascination with my alter-ego.

Sir –

The writer presumes that you will kindly overlook the liberty he has taken in addressing a few lines on the subject of the so-called "Spring Heeled Jack panic" that has caused much alarming sensation in the Surrey township of Guildford.

It appears that some individual (of, the writer believes, the lowest and most unmanly sort) has taken upon himself the guise of a spectre or demon in order to engage in base thievery and mischievous pranks. It is high time that such a detestable nuisance should be put a stop to, and the writer seeks assurance that soon the authorities will exert their utmost power to bring the villain to justice.

Sir –

I regret that I must take issue with those of your esteemed correspondents who insist that Spring Heeled Jack's nefarious activities are restricted to the Southern provinces. I hail from rural Yorkshire and I well remember Jack from my youth. My own cousin once beheld this ghost or devil, leaping over tall hedges and cottages in the moonlight and laughing like a lunatic. As he sped off he called out, "the day is yours – leave the night to me!"

(I confess that I rather liked that line, and so committed it to memory.)

Sir –

Perhaps yourself or your readers may be in the position to confirm, or otherwise, the rumour that "Spring Heeled Jack" is in fact an inventor from London, experimenting with some new form of flying machine. My neighbour's maid saw him not two days ago, sailing straight past an open window on the second story of her master's home, whereupon the poor girl had been so started as to drop a very valuable tea-set, which shattered upon the floor.

Sir –

It seems rather too much of a co-incidence that, in both cases of Spring Heeled Jack's appearances in the vicinity of Guildford, he has battled with men in the employ of Sir Roland of Ashton Hall. Is there any truth to the rumour that His Lordship now fears for his own safety and that this is the reason for his forthcoming departure to his London estate?

I shall admit now that I had written the latter inquiry myself, under the pseudonym "Jack Barnestable." We had received word that Roland was preparing to return to London for an extended business trip. Fortunately for young Lanigan, with the entire town of Guildford having witnessed Jack in action, his testimony was now redundant and Ned's contacts confirmed that my cousin would not pursue him any further. Ned and I would follow close behind Roland, for our mission was yet scarcely started, and in the meantime I could not resist guying him via the newspapers.

In fact, I knew that my cousin was too canny not to have realised by then that the Spring Heeled Jack was a weapon aimed in his direction, though of course he could not have begun to suspect the identity of the man behind the Devil's mask.

Chapter 14

En route back to London Town in pursuit of my perfidious cousin, Ned and I made an excursion to the site of the Medmenham Abbey, towards gaining some insight into the activities of the Hellfire Club. The trip took most of the day and we stopped for the evening at an inn in the village of High Wycombe.

Taking our dinner in the tavern, we discovered the landlord, a Mr. Chesney, to be a most gregarious fellow, full of stories about the strange goings-on at the Abbey when Dashwood and his fellow free-thinkers had made it their headquarters, nearly a hundred years previously. Ned asked questions whilst I remained in the background and, of course, in disguise, against the chance that talk of the Hellfire Club might attract unwelcome attention.

"They say that once, Sir Francis let loose a baboon in the Church on Sunday," Chesney confided to Ned, "and the panic that caused, well I'm sure you can imagine, Sir. Folk thought it was the Devil himself come to visit, or at least an imp. And then there were the orgies, if you'll pardon me, but we're all red-blooded men here, and the 'Nuns of Medmenham' weren't all fallen women, I can tell you that. There were some high born ladies amongst them."

"I've heard tell of caverns beneath the Abbey. Mr. Chesney," prompted Ned. "Some sort of cod-heathen business with a river and such?"

"Oh, there's no river under there, Mr. Burrage, never was. You can still get into most of the caves but they're dark and dreary places now. We used to play in them when we were lads, my brothers and me, and all round here of our vintage. It's a shame really, what's become of the Abbey. Just lots of old stones and stories these days."

He talked on and it became evident that as far as the people of High Wycombe were concerned, the Abbey and the Hellfire Club were merely colourful features of their local history. This was confirmed the next day when we visited the Abbey, which was almost disappointingly easy to find, being well sign-posted from the village.

It was a once-magnificent but now sadly neglected edifice. We could easily make out the architectural additions Dashwood had made upon his purchase of the property - mock-Classical follies, overgrown grottoes and such - and a weathered engraving of the Hellfire Club motto over one of the doors brought a wry smile to my lips. *Fay ce que voudras* ... though certainly the life of Spring Heeled Jack, highwayman and gentleman adventurer, was not quite what Abbot Holt and his shadow council had in mind for me. Unfortunately, no clue as to what they might have in mind for me was available in the ruins of Medmenham.

We investigated the caves beneath as well, but although their aesthetic was vaguely similar to that of the caverns where I had recuperated and had my bizarre encounter with the Clubmen in their guising masks, their layout was quite different. Also, from their state of disrepair and neglect, it was quite obvious that the Medmenham caves had not been visited for years, other than by children at bold play and, going by the scatalogical nature of some of the graffiti on the walls, by young men larking about. Certainly there was no sign of the whimsical/sinister decorations that had festooned the other caves, nor, as Mr. Chesney had asserted, of the subterranean river I had crossed.

In all, although I perceived a certain sympathy between the Medmenham caverns and those in which I had been sequestered, perhaps indicative of that between the Hellfire Club of Dashwood's day and that of our own, this visit confirmed my suspicion that the modern Club had shifted its headquarters. We proceeded to London, refreshed by the outing but none the wiser about the men who had saved my life, in their own highly mysterious fashion.

Chapter 15

Upon returning to the city, I took the precaution of establishing three separate identities at different railway hotels – nothing too ostentatious, of course – but with the tactical aim of surrounding Ashton House at Soho Square, where Roland had made his metropolitan headquarters. Thus, I hoped to track his comings and goings, his business dealings, and gain such intelligence as might force him, perhaps through blackmail, into confessing his perjury against me.

Posing as "Jack Shaw", booked in to the new Langham Hotel, I was a civil engineer. This Marylebone hotel was equipped with a hydraulic lift machine, which was a source of fascination and amusement to Mr. Shaw. Architect "Jack Geoffreys" paid a month's rent in advance for the privilege of staying at the Great Eastern in Liverpool Street, whilst "Jack Haining", a writer seeking inspiration in the great city, was sequestered at the Charing Cross Hotel. Meanwhile, Ned had returned to gainful self-employment as a Hanson cab driver, ever with an ear out for news of Roland's dealings.

We also prepared another, far less conventional lodging place, against the chance that any or all of these identities might have to disappear at a moment's notice. I well recalled the crypt in the long-abandoned Wardour Street graveyard where I had retrieved my boots and other sundries from the garroter and his drab, and Ned and I made several trips there under cover of darkness.

We secured access to the mausoleum, a somber and dignified building that had evidently not been visited for the best part of a hundred years, by prising up one of the marble flag-stones that comprised its roof. Ned contrived an ingenious pivot mechanism that allowed the stone to rotate, revealing an opening that either of us might slip through. Within the crypt, which extended for some distance underground, we concealed a supply of money, lanterns, changes of clothes, cots and such other necessities as might be required by a fugitive in the heart of London. Should the Hellfire Club, the police, Roland or any other adversary force our hand, we had at least one bolt-hole well prepared.

It became my habit to trail my cousin during his excursions about the city, occasionally in my various earthly disguises and at street level during the day, and more frequently as the Spring Heeled Jack across the rooftops of an evening. By so doing, I was able to accustom myself to navigating the roof-scape, and soon sailing across London alleyways and scaling hotel walls felt as natural as riding a horse. The exercise kept me in excellent trim and revealed to me that upper-world of London that was normally haunt only to pigeons and chimney-sweeps.

At this time I had occasion to modify my equipment, for so many of the rooftops were steeply gabled that I found myself climbing as often as running and jumping. After a close call one night, when I slipped and nearly skidded off the brink of a four-story building, I added two sharp spurs to the toes and heels of my shoe-platforms, and two spiked prongs to the inside edges of my gauntlets. I soon became adept at forking these in between roofing tiles and wooden slats. With considerable effort, I was even able to scale vertical walls for short distances.

I also discovered the full potentials and limitations of my spring-stilts, and learned that whereas I could comfortably clear a twenty-foot gap between two level rooftops with a running start, or while jumping from a roof to a lower surface, I had no hope of crossing such a distance while leaping upwards.

The maximum height I could spring up from a crouching start seemed to be eight feet. Conversely, the extraordinary tensile properties of the springs allowed me to drop a good two and one half stories without injury, once I had mastered the knack of employing my cape as a sort of parachute and flexing my knees just so to absorb the shock of landing. Dropping from such a height to the street and instantly rebounding, I could reliably bounce back up to the roof of a two-story building.

Occasionally I was puzzled by what I found up on the roofs – objects such as small carts and items of weather-beaten furniture that seemed to have no rightful place there, and odd markings scratched into the soot of chimney flues. Twice during those first weeks, as I bounded high above the streets, I would have sworn that I had heard whispering voices and soft whistles from the shadows. Still, this I put down to the sighs and moans of the wind as it set weather-vanes a-spin and howled down open gratings.

Then, upon an evening's jaunt across the roofscape surrounding Covent Garden, attempting to stay ahead of my perfidious cousin's carriage, I was startled to be hailed with a piercing whistle. I came up short and spun, glancing all about the rooftop, but could see no-one in the shadows.

"Are you the Devil?"

A child's voice!

"Where are you?" I asked.

"Hiding." Whispers and muttering from the dark.

"Are you really the Devil, only we've seen you jump and Megark doesn't think you're a man." Another apparently disembodied voice, perhaps a girl's.

"I'm a man dressed up as the Devil. Where are you, child?"

There was a brief silence, then more whispers in some sort of bizarre cant. I made out something that sounded like "hegell dewskitch egus".

"We won't come out because we don't know what you'll do to us."

Somewhere on this rooftop high above Kingsway, against all reason, there were at least three young children.

"I will not hurt you."

There was more gibberish conversation from the shadows.

"The other one does when he sees us."

"What other one? Do you mean another man like me?"

There was silence, but they had my full attention. I would humour them and see where it led.

"Will you do some jumps for us?" asked one of them.

"If I show you some jumps, you must repay me. Will you show yourselves?"

Suddenly I was aware of movement behind me and I turned, not so quickly as might startle them. There were three children crouched in the shadows next to the ledge. I doubted that any were older than twelve years, though it was hard to tell either ages or genders as all were dressed in layers of ragged wool and cotton and caked with soot from head to toe – a most effective camouflage. Their clothing and caps were crudely decorated with numerous pigeon feathers stitched into the fabric. Then another two crept out from beneath a shallow overhang very close to me. All but the smallest held catapults with thick India rubber bands stretched taut.

"All right, then," the tallest girl said. She and the others sat upon the ledge and I obliged them with some fancy leaps, springing at one point over their heads and over to the next rooftop, from whence I took a short run-up and turned a tight somersault back over the gap, landing before them again. At this they applauded politely, for all the world like little ladies and gentlemen out for a Sunday stroll, impressed by some street acrobat's tricks.

"Can we do that?" asked one of the boys.

"No, you would need to be grown up, and I have special boots. Please, tell me how you come to be here."

In short order, I learned that the children called themselves the "Shivering Jemmies" and that most had escaped the brutal life of servitude as a chimney-sweep's apprentice, but that there were others amongst them, including girls, who had escaped from workhouses and chosen to live on the rooftops rather than in the streets. All were either orphaned or simply did not know where their parents were.

The tallest and presumably eldest of them was a girl who said that her name was Jegane. She reported that she and her friends subsisted on what they could steal by descending into wealthy homes through their chimneys, which she and the others called "chimbleys", and they made their lairs in long-forgotten attics and belfries across the city. They went down to street level only when absolutely necessary.

Occasionally as they spoke to me they would squabble amongst themselves over some point and break into their curious cant, and I took this to be a cypher-language used to conceal the subject of their conversation from outsiders. At a guess, it combined rhyming slang with some sort of Pig Latin, liberally sprinkled with Gypsy words; certainly, I could not begin to follow it.

They said that they sometimes traded information, such as the layout of wealthy homes, to adult thieves, in return for money, drink and tobacco. With their catapults they hunted pigeons and squirrels for sport and, sometimes, food.

Next there was some talk of "wars" between their little gang and another, "the Snakesmen" who occupied other territories, which seemed to be defined by those buildings clustered sufficiently closely together to be easily traversed without descending to the street. They had established routes, tying short lengths of rope to aid in climbing the steeper gables and secreting planks behind the guttering at points where they could be strung between two buildings in close proximity. I was reminded of the curious objects I had sometimes encountered on the rooftops, and wondered how many of London's orphans had taken to this strange life.

It was evidently a hard and dangerous existence, but, they asserted, it was better than the squalor of the tenements and the lot of a pickpocket or sweep's apprentice. Up here they made their own rules and answered only to each other.

The children seemed to take to me and pointed out one of their lairs nearby, a rickety old belfry that was just visible in the gloom, several streets away. I must confess that I was impressed by the "Jemmies" and also fearful for them, but when at last they made off across the roofs they moved like cats, quite silent and bold in their agility. I could but hope that Spring Heeled Jack had made some allies that night.

Chapter 16

My conniving cousin Roland kept largely to himself, travelling when necessary to one or two gentlemen's clubs and to the theatre or opera. He was evidently a creature of habit, and over the course of a fortnight he established a fairly regular schedule and assortment of haunts throughout the city. The furthest from Ashton House he ever seemed inclined to travel was the gymnasium attached to the Inns of Court, where he was partial to taking exercise.

Whenever he went, perhaps mindful of Spring Heeled Jack, he was accompanied by several bodyguards who made the Surrey rent-men look like the bumpkins they were. His London guards were great burly bravos stuffed into suits, all, I was sure, armed to the very teeth.

As I became accustomed to the role of the "ghost or Devil", I grew bold enough to make my presence felt to Roland and his men directly. One evening I sprang down into the path of his carriage and thence to a shop awning across the road, there pausing to squat, gargoylishly. The driver pulled his steeds up sharply, cursing, and then shouted an alarm.

When I saw Roland's face appear at the carriage window I raised my gauntleted right hand and pointed at him. I could not decide whether his expression was panicked or simply furious; and then I had no time for guessing, as the driver proceeded to draw a pistol from his heavy coat. I was away again before he could take proper aim, bouncing off the roof of the carriage, and I was pleased to hear Roland's response to this, though I shall not now repeat it.

All of this gallivanting about the heights made marvellous newspaper copy as, inevitably, I was not infrequently spotted by pedestrians and I often startled respectable families and office-dwellers by sailing past their windows. Between us, Ned and I kept up the hobby of collecting newspaper reports and editorials concerning the exploits of Spring Heeled Jack, which we would keep until such time as we could add them to his scrapbook, which he left secreted away in the crypt.

The "Jack" of the newspapers was being spotted with increasing frequency throughout the length and breadth of England, though most especially, and most truly, in central London. Elsewhere, he seemed to have nothing better to do than to startle farmers by bounding across lonely moors or to make the occasional leap over garden walls to grope innocent serving maids.

In terms of appearance, he was variously described as a shrouded ghost, a fire-spitting and skull-faced demon, "a bear" by one nine-year-old witness, and, in another memorable instance, as a knight in full armour wearing red shoes. Some of the London reports, though, were accurate enough.

Spring-heeled Jack. Awful representation of the London monster.

An awful representation, indeed …

Ned found great amusement in all of this and made a game of judging whether a given report was most likely to represent a true sighting, a prankish imitator or a confabulation. For my part, I wondered again whether the Hellfire Club had yet made the connection between Jack Ashton and "the Leaping Demon of Soho."

One Thursday morning we were given pause by an unusual and disturbing item from the nearby district of Bow, reported in the normally sober *London Times*:

Outrage at Old Ford

The Spring-Heeled Jack Strikes Again

At about a quarter to nine o'clock (...) Miss Jane Alsop heard a violent ringing at the gate at the front of the house, and on going to the door to see what was the matter, she saw a man standing outside, of whom she enquired what was the matter, and requested he would not ring so loud. The person instantly replied that he was a policeman, and said 'For God's sake, bring me a light, for we have caught Spring-heeled Jack here in the lane.' She returned into the house and brought a candle, and handed it to the person, who appeared enveloped in a long cloak, and whom she at first really believed to be a policeman.

The instant she had done so, however, he threw off his outer garment, and applying the lighted candle to his breast, presented a most hideous and frightful appearance, and vomited forth a quantity of blue and white flames from his mouth, and his eyes resembled red balls of fire. From the hasty glance, which her fright enabled her to get of his person, she observed that he wore a large helmet, and his dress, which appeared to fit him very tight, seemed to her to resemble white oilskin.

Without uttering a sentence, he darted at her, and catching her partly by her dress and the back part of her neck, placed her head under one of his arms, and commenced tearing her gown with his claws, which she was certain were of some metallic substance. She screamed out as loud as she could for assistance, and by considerable exertion got away from him, and ran towards the house to get in.

Her assailant, however, followed her, and caught her on the steps leading to the half-door, when he again used considerable violence, tore her neck and arms with his claws, as well as a quantity of hair from her head; but she was at length rescued from his grasp by one of her sisters. Miss Alsop added, that she had suffered considerably all night from the shock she had sustained, and was then in extreme pain, both from the injury done to her arm, and the wounds and scratches inflicted by the miscreant about her shoulders and neck with his claws or hands."

Amidst all the nonsense and increasingly hysterical speculation as to the identity and activities of Spring Heeled Jack, this appeared to have been a genuine and serious assault, and it was reported with due gravity. The article further mentioned that the Anti-Garroting Societies – armed vigilante groups dedicated to patrolling the streets against the sort of attack that had been made upon me in Soho – were taking a keen interest in the case and would be focussing their attentions on Bow for the immediate future.

Further, a committee of concerned and wealthy citizens, shocked at this brazen and bizarre assault upon a girl from a good family, in her own home, had formed to contribute funds and aid in any way they could.

A few days later, another, similar report featured in the Times. This concerned the misadventure that had befallen an eighteen-year old girl named Lucy Scales, a butcher's daughter from Limehouse, and her sister Margaret. The young ladies had apparently been accosted by a man or monster fitting the description given by Miss Alsop, whilst walking in the streets near their home. The assault had taken place at a quarter of nine in the evening.

Again, mention was made of the assailant's long cloak and of his having belched fire into his victim's face; in this case, the unfortunate Lucy had been blinded for some hours, her face disfigured and hair burnt by the flames, and she had been sent into a fit of hysterics. Neither girl was able to say from whence the attacker had come, nor how he had escaped, but Margaret was quoted as saying, "He was not there one moment, and then the next, there he was. I heard not a sound until he pounced at Lucy."

This was rum stuff indeed, and it gave me pause to wonder whether my penny dreadful guise and exploits had somehow offered artistic license to baser villains. I would never hope to claim that my motives were purely altruistic, and do not to this very day; I intended justice done for my own part, and damned be any man who crossed me in that. Yet, I shall readily admit that it rankled that some vicious criminal might somehow borrow from my ingenuity, molesting innocent young girls and thereby tarnishing "Jack's" reputation. If nothing else, it had the potential to make my task of tracking and harassing Roland all the more difficult. I resolved to keep an eye on these stories.

Chapter 17

One Saturday evening, as I was skimming across the roofs and following Roland's coach back from the School of Arms, I spied one of the guards alight from the carriage and bid those within a gruff good evening. Upon a whim, I followed the man as he made his way through the winding alleyways of Soho towards the nearest public house. With a mind to visit the fellow and test the mettle of my cousin's new bravos, I sprang onto the tavern roof and hid in the shadow of the chimney-stack, awaiting his departure.

Some little while later I heard movement and hushed voices from the rear of the building. Sure enough, there was the very man I had been trailing, now slightly the worse for drink, pawing at a serving woman in the courtyard below.

"I must get back," the wench protested, though none too vehemently. "The owner'll be missing me and I do have a living to earn, you know. Unlike some!"

"I told you, lovely, I'm employed. I mind a well-to-do gent, a Lord, he is." The brute's voice was deep and slurred.

"Wait, do, I'll be back in a moment." The woman pulled free of him and disappeared from my sight, back towards the pub. This was the moment, and I prepared to make my entrance as the man below ambled towards far end of the yard, evidently intending to relieve himself against the high brick wall.

He approached a ramshackle gate leading out of the yard and glanced about from side to side into the alley beyond and then upwards, whereupon he seemed to stagger as if struck a blow. He stood frozen for a moment before giving a great, anguished cry and then, reeling and retching, he stumbled back towards the pub. From my vantage point on the roof I could not see what had caused this strange behaviour, and so as he disappeared below me I sprang quickly down into the courtyard and then vaulted over the wall beyond, alighting in the dim alleyway.

At first I could make out nothing untoward other than what appeared to be a heap of ash or sand a little way along to my right, but then I heard a spattering sound as if an icicle was melting, and as I turned I felt droplets upon my mask. I looked upward and beheld such a grisly sight as I shall never forget.

A woman's body was hanging headfirst from beneath a wooden balcony some thirty feet over the paving, her arms dangling, and blood was dripping from her fingertips to the cobbles below. As I watched, her fingers twitched weakly.

In an instant, I heard the sound of a Peeler's rattle from down the alley and raised voices from behind me, as people came running out of the tavern. I knew that I must seek the heights again. As I prepared to leap away, I was struck with a terrible dilemma – the poor wretch above was still alive, having suffered some awful accident or bizarre foul-play. Spring Heeled Jack was sure to take the blame should he be spotted nearby, yet I could not simply leave the woman. I stood frozen for a moment, in an agony of indecision, and then just as the constable rounded the far corner to my right, I knew that the chance to save a life must outweigh "Jack's" reputation.

With a straight leap upwards and a scramble I gained the top of the brick wall, perhaps ten feet in height. As the Peeler ran in below me, I sprang from the wall to a nearby scaffold and from thence across the alley and over the railing of the balcony, which shifted and creaked as I alighted upon it.

The doors that must have once have opened out onto this dismal spot had obviously been long since boarded up, and the wood of the balcony itself seemed dangerously rotten. I saw at once the rough hemp rope from which the woman was suspended, tied off against a rusted iron hook embedded in the wall. I peered over the decaying balustrade, not wishing to chance my weight against it, and called out to the Peeler down below:

"You, there! She is alive, but barely; I dare not haul her up, for the wood is rotten. If I let the rope out, can you catch her?"

"Who are you, and what have you done?" the constable shouted up at me. "I'll have others here in a moment, you shan't escape!" He spun his rattle again, the loud ratcheting noise echoing through the alley.

The balcony gave a sudden, shuddering lurch away from its moorings and I knew that there was no time to argue with the man.

"I am Spring Heeled Jack, and this woman will surely die unless we save her! I will cut the rope and let her down as best I can. You must be ready to catch her, do you hear?"

At this point his voice was joined by others, presumably patrons of the tavern.

"Let her down, blast you!" the Peeler cried out.

"Who is that up there?" asked another man.

"It's the demon, Springle Jack!"

Cursing that I had no proper knife, I braced against the rope, winding what slack I could about my body, and began to saw at the rope with my right gauntlet, spurs of steel slicing the tiny fibres until the taut cord snapped. I was swung about by the woman's falling weight and the balcony shifted again with a splintering wrench, pulling free of the wall entirely at the far end and skewing out at a drunken angle over the alley. I could not see what was happening below and had scarcely more than five feet of rope to lower. Wrapping the frayed end of the rope about my wrist and calling upon all my faculties of strength and balance, I let her down until I could stretch no further.

"She's too high, we can't reach her!" came the policeman's voice from below, at which moment the balcony gave one final groan and swung out and down again, broken timbers crashing into the brick wall on the other side of the alley, where they wedged in place. I heard the gathering crowd gasp and scatter as bits of rotten wood and rusted nails rained upon them. Still, fortune had gained us another precious seven feet, and moments later I felt the weight eased from my right arm.

"I have her now," the constable called out. "Oh, Lord, the blood … awful …"

I climbed quickly from the balcony to the top of the brick wall, glowering down into a mass of faces, some frightened and some fascinated, while the constable and two other men carried the woman a little way down the alley.

"There he is!" came a cry from the pressing crowd. I had to be away from there, and quickly. At that very instant, the supporting planks gave out and the whole structure collapsed down in a cacophony of shrieking timbers and panicked cries from below. Knowing that I could do nothing else for the victim, I leaped down into the courtyard, sending onlookers scrambling and screaming, then back up to the tavern roof and away into the night.

Chapter 18

By the next evening, the bizarre and gruesome events in that Soho back-alley had become the talk of London. The Times reported that the poor woman, a twenty-one year old seamstress whose name was Polly Brown, had died due to loss of blood mere hours afterward. Her face was said to have been badly burned, to the extent that her eyes had been poached in their sockets. She had also received numerous deep gouges to her hands, neck, back and chest, as if she had been mauled by some great jungle beast.

Of course, the report noted that Spring Heeled Jack was widely assumed to have done the grisly deed himself, but it also mentioned a quieter rumour insisting that the girl had attempted to take her own life and that Jack had tried to save her, at his own peril.

I met with Ned in the lantern-lit crypt beneath St. Anne's Churchyard and related what had happened from my own perspective.

Ned mused, "Folk on the streets are saying she was a suicide, Cap'n – but I can't see it, not 'appening like that. I reckon someone hung 'er there."

"I'm inclined to agree. And beyond that, there is a pattern in these recent reports; the victims were all young women, there was the matter of fiery breath in both prior cases, and the mention of clawed hands in one. Polly Brown's face was burned, and she had been cut or clawed to death. These are not foolish pranks nor tall tales, Ned; I warrant that the Alsop and Scales attacks were the work of a man testing his mettle, building himself up to killing that poor young girl last night. God knows how long she had hung there, blind and helpless, before I got her down."

"The bastard!" Ned's eyes narrowed and both hands knotted into fists. As gruff as he could be, the old Sergeant - who had no children of his own - felt deeply for the plight of London's most vulnerable young denizens, and shared my contempt for any man who would so abuse his strength as to molest or injure an innocent young girl. "We must put a stop to 'im, Cap'n, and soon; the Peelers 'ave their ways, but we 'ave ours."

"Aye, fellow. But how to bring the villain to bay?"

Ned puffed on his pipe furiously, deep in thought.

"The thing that strikes me is, how did the blackguard get her up there in the first place?" he mused. "Ye said there was no access to that balcony from within the building."

"The roof above, I'd warrant. The drop from roof to balcony was in the order of thirty feet, straight down."

"So – the villain burns and cuts 'er, p'rhaps up on the roof, though Lord knows how they got up there, then drops or lowers the poor lass down by rope and climbs after 'er to finish the job."

"It seems the only possible explanation, but why? Why go to so much trouble?"

"I reckon the mad-man has a point to make, Cap'n. Also, if ye'll pardon me, 'ow long until Peelers are stationed up on the roofs, once 'tis known that this assassin is hidin' up there? An' 'ow many of them would know or care to pick between yer good self and the lunatic, before shooting?

Yer cousin's not changin' his ways about the city. I can keep tabs on him for you, free you to track down the Hellfire Club and put a stop to this lunatic fer good an' all."

The canny old soldier was right; I could not afford to exhaust myself, and as long as the murderer was known to be using the roofs of London, my own mission against Roland was at even greater risk.

By the same token, and this was something that I had not hitherto given enough credit: Roland showed every sign of conducting himself as a respectable man about town. Despite weeks of trailing his every move, we had gathered no evidence that might be used to blackmail him; I still had no leverage short of physical force that might encourage his confession, nor any reason to imagine that a confession, thus extracted, would secure the rightful claim of Jack Ashton, recently hanged traitor to the Crown.

For all that Spring Heeled Jack might be able to irritate and intimidate "Sir" Roland Ashton and his bravos, the harsh truth was that without the backing of the Hellfire Club as to my true identity, I had no sure means of reclaiming my title and lands. It was even possible that, given the time that had passed, the Club would now "have need of me", as I recalled Brother Farmara saying.

"You're quite right, Sergeant. I shall leave my cousin to your surveillance, and focus on these other matters for the time being."

Upon our map marked with Roland's travels and haunts, we imposed a new set of marks, representing the assaults at Bow and Limehouse and the murder, as we felt sure it was, in Soho.

It was then that I recalled the efforts by private parties that were already in place – the Anti-Garroting Societies, and the committee of concerned citizens. I proposed that Ned should join one of the vigilante groups, whilst "Jack Haining", my journalistic alter-ego, infiltrated the committee. Between us, we stood a better chance of gathering such intelligence as might lead the real Spring Heeled Jack to his vicious impersonator.

Ned had a word of caution for me.

"D'ye think it wise to get so close to the Peelers, Sir? They're surely after the murderer, but so many believe yerself and him to be one and the same man."

"What's one more chance, my friend?" We shook hands and emerged from the crypt under cover of inky darkness, two men dedicated to the Devil's means in service of a greater good.

Chapter 19

The next day "Jack Haining" made some inquiries via the Charing Cross hotel management and discovered that the citizens' committee, which had taken upon itself the name of "the Wellingtonians", after the late Duke, was to meet at seven o'clock that very night. This rendezvous was to be held at the Alfred Club in Albemarle Street.

An hour before the meeting was due to take place, I was standing in the well-appointed bar of the Alfred Club and chatting with their President, the rotund and convivial Mr. Frederick Barnes of Barnes and Wiley Publishing. Upon learning that Jack Haining was an up and coming writer, Barnes exerted his considerable charm in persuading me to join the Club as a full member.

"Young blood, Mr. Haining, and vigour – that is what the Club needs! Between you and I, most Clubmen have much more money than vim. As a member you will also have access to our library for your research – it is held in some regard in scholarly circles, I believe - and a quiet place to compose your thoughts."

"That would be welcome indeed, Mr. Barnes. I shall give this some serious consideration."

"Pish, what's to consider! I'll tell you what, I shall vouch for you myself to speed things along."

At that, Mr. Barnes excused himself to prepare for the meeting of the Wellingtonian Society. After a few moments I followed him into the Club's meeting room, which was already near-full, and found a seat.

After a few preliminaries, Barnes officially opened the meeting by welcoming us all and started to expound upon the establishment's history. He was cut short by a peevish gentleman sitting behind me, who demanded, to general murmurs of agreement, that we should get down to business. Barnes handled the interjection with aplomb and passed the chair over to Inspector Charles Lea, who was introduced as being the chief police officer in charge of the "Spring Heeled Jack" case. As Lea took the podium the audience hushed immediately, for his name was famous throughout England, his father, James, having cracked several sensational cases in the '30s.

Charles Lea had an imposing presence, dark of hair and eye and bearing a prominent, aquiline nose. He was attended by a constable and by a young woman, presumably his secretary or wife, whose presence must have been by special dispensation of the Chairman, as the Alfred Club was normally barred to members of the fair sex. Lea's manner was both serious and vigorous as he commenced to address the assembly.

"Thank you, Mr. Barnes. Gentlemen, I shall not beat about the bush; the recent events connected to the criminal known as Spring Heeled Jack are of great concern to all of us, most especially those with young daughters, nieces and sisters resident in London and the surrounding villages. I am authorised to inform you that the case of Miss Polly Brown is now being treated as a murder investigation."

There was some consternation at this; as Ned had reported, the prevailing public opinion had been that Miss Brown had committed suicide, with the Spring Heeled Jack's role in the affair being the subject of much confusion and debate.

Lea went on to state that the police believed the attacks upon Jane Alsop and Lucy Scales to have been committed by the same fiend who had murdered Polly Brown, so in that their hypothesis agreed with my own. He continued:

"We are hampered simultaneously by a lack of evidence pertaining directly to these cases, and by an over-abundance of rumour and speculation amongst the press and the general public. Gentlemen, you are all educated men and I shall speak frankly; this is no ghost, nor demon that we are dealing with. He is a man, most likely a meticulous and intelligent sort, but highly dangerous and subject to the worst forms of depravity. We believe that he will continue to strike until he is captured."

At that moment there was some movement at the rear of the assembly room, and I turned to behold my cousin Roland, accompanied by two of his bodyguards, enter and take seats towards the rear. They sat at such an angle from me that I could shield my profile from their view with slight turn of the head and a hand casually raised to my chin; I hoped that these precautions and the mass of people in the room would be enough to conceal me from his attention.

Inspector Lea referred to his papers.

"Our present problem," he went on, "is simply that our resources are being stretched in distinguishing fact from fiction, mistaken identity, and what the alienists call "playing the ghost". The latter is a peculiar mania that sparks the imaginations of some persons, causing them to disguise themselves and so then to imitate famous hauntings and the like.

Frankly, much of this is, if not innocent, then at least only of nuisance value. Not three days ago a pack of school-boys in the North were instrumental in the capture of a local "Spring Heeled Jack" whose only alleged crime seems to have been in leaping out and startling people. And that is part of our present dilemma; there are Spring Heeled Jacks popping up here, there and everywhere. Most of them are just young bucks with more vim than sense, but this one man is extremely dangerous."

At this point an elderly fellow seated in the front row raised his hand to be allowed to speak.

"Is there any truth, to the best of your knowledge, in the rumour that the killer might be a man of a higher station in life? Specifically, I have heard about some wager laid by a group of aristocrats, to the effect that one of them should dress up as this Springle Jack and thereby literally get away with murder!"

At this suggestion there was a considerable uproar, and the old man continued:

"I have here a sketch of the miscreant from one of the provincial papers, which I will gladly pass about for any man here to see."

Spring Heeled Jack as imagined by a *Middlesbrough Daily Gazette* sketch artist.

At this, Lea raised his hands for silence.

"We have heard that rumour, Sir, but at this stage we can give it no more credence than any other. It would explain certain details but we have no firm evidence leading us to the conclusion that the killer is a gentleman, if I may use that term very loosely."

"My wife's brother - a man I hold in the highest esteem - heard that this villain may be associated in some way with the Fleet Street disappearances …" began another man.

"I can confirm that we have no evidence to that effect, Sir," Lea replied smoothly.

Then came a hectoring voice that I instantly recognised as Roland's, from the rear of the room:

"And what about the recent attacks in Surrey, Mr. Lea? I can assure you that they were neither imaginary, nor mere school-boy pranks."

"Our investigators have cause to doubt that the same man was involved in the Surrey and London attacks. It is possible that the London assailant is amongst those inspired by the Surrey highwayman, but again, all of this is speculative at this stage.

There is also the fact, and I wish to underscore this point, that a significant number of witnesses to the tragedy in Soho, including one of my constables, insist that the Spring Heeled Jack who appeared there last night was, in fact, attempting to rescue the poor young woman. If so, that would be odd behaviour indeed for a murderer."

Lea referred to his papers once again and took a deep breath before continuing.

"Gentlemen, I appeal to you on behalf of the Metropolitan Police. You are men of wealth and influence in the city and the last thing London needs is a full-blown panic. Please, exert whatever powers you can to calm the situation, whether through the newspapers, as leaders of your local communities, or in lending a firm guiding hand to the vigilante crews.

Dr. Roberts, our chief alienist and a most perceptive judge of the human psyche, suggests that now that a real villain has committed this atrocity, the number of Spring Heeled Jack imitators will quickly dwindle. In the mean-time, of course, we can use any able-bodied and clear-headed men to assist us with our investigations. I thank you all for your kind attention."

At a signal from Inspector Lea, the young constable who had been standing unobtrusively beside Mr. Barnes throughout, passed amongst the audience handing out sheets of paper. These provided a summary of Lea's main points and other notes pertaining to the case, including contact addresses for himself and other key figures involved in the police investigation. Further down were listed the editorial addresses of every major newspaper and the names of the constables who were liasing with the various local vigilante societies.

I was most impressed by Lea's foresight and professionalism and determined to assist in any way I could. Of course, my methods would not quite match what he had in mind. I waited until Roland and his henchmen had departed before standing to make my own exit, resolved that Spring Heeled Jack should mount his own investigation of the rooftop above the balcony in Soho, that very night.

I was about to leave when Frederick Barnes hailed me from across the floor.

"Mr. Haining? I say, Sir!"

I turned and found myself face to face with Charles Lea.

"Mr. Haining, so glad I could catch you," Barnes began. "Of course this is Inspector Lea, and may I also introduce his charming sister, Catherine."

I composed myself as well as I could and murmured the appropriate 'delighted-to-meet-yous", as Barnes went on:

"Mr. Haining here is a writer, and the Inspector was just asking if we had any of those handy, so to speak."

"Well, I am at your service, of course, Inspector, although I fear that most of my writing is of a hobbyist nature at present." This was dangerous; I had written nothing at all as Jack Haining, little enough even under my own name other than letters and some frankly mediocre poetry, and Lea was as sharp as a tack.

"Oh, I'm sure that Mr. Haining is far too modest," said Lea's sister, with a gracious smile. I had guessed wrongly about their relationship and now had occasion to notice the similarity of their features, Catherine's aquiline nose, not so prominent as her brother's, the same dark hair and intelligent green eyes.

"The project that we have in mind is this," said Lea. "The organisation of the Wellingtonians is a novel concept, and I can see that a party of educated and influential men, prepared to take an active stand against crime, should be of great benefit to the Metropolitan Police and to the city itself. I was wondering if you would be prepared to take up the editorship of a new broadsheet, which I've thought to call the 'Wellingtonian Gazette'. Its purpose would be similar to that of these meetings, to keep the members abreast of any current cases of interest, advancements in alienism, criminology and so-on."

My mind raced to consider the implications of Lea's offer. As Ned had cautioned me, it was risky to get so close to the Police, even though Jack Haining could, more or less, vanish from the face of the Earth simply by checking out of his hotel. On the other hand, this project might be of great help in my own covert investigations.

"Mr. Barnes has offered to handle all of the printing and so-forth, so your role would be as an overseer, perhaps helping to frame the articles produced by our staff in a way that is accessible to the educated layman," Lea continued. "Of course, you would be paid a stipend for your time and expertise. I would have to say that you'd be offering us all a great service, Mr. Haining."

"Well then, it shall be my pleasure to accept."

Lea smiled and offered a firm handshake, and Barnes seemed equally delighted, offering to seal the deal with another round of drinks at the bar. All the while, a voice within me, much reminiscent of Ned's, muttered darkly of untoward risk.

Chapter 20

The New English Opera House faced into Dean Street and was easily accessible, for me at least, via the neighbouring building. Its roof was a gently gabled expanse, featureless other than two large, three-chimneyed stacks and a beam supporting a pulley hoist on the far side.

By the light of a shuttered lantern, I carefully studied the stack nearest to the rear wall above the former balcony, and noted with grim satisfaction that a patch of soot had been recently rubbed away, very much as if by someone tying a rope about it. Corresponding marks on the edge of the roof seemed to confirm Ned's theory that the villain had lowered Miss Brown, and likely himself, down onto the balcony. The rooftop was also marred by a dark stain, obviously dried blood, which likewise led erratically from the area about the chimney stack to the edge of the roof.

In all, it was a perfect location for a brutal assault and murder; the lofty height both preventing anyone from witnessing the deed and offering the victim no means of escape.

I blew out the lantern, leaned against the stack and gazed out over the moonlit roof-scape of Soho, trying to piece the puzzle together. How had the murderer gotten himself and his victim up to this desolate spot? I recalled the scaffolding set up against the building to the rear of the Opera House, next door to the tavern, but a mere glance told me that access via that route would have been impossible, as the scaffold reached barely a third of the necessary height.

Lea's broadsheet had mentioned one detail that had been missing in the press reports, namely that Miss Brown was thought to have been walking in the area close to where her body was found. I circumnavigated the perimeter, but there were no ladders, and the seemingly derelict fire escape platforms on the East side did not approach the height of the rooftop. Even if they had, I could not conceive of the man who could snatch a young, healthy girl from street level and carry her by ladder to such a height, surely not without attracting some attention. Had she been disabled, perhaps rendered unconscious, or intimidated into making the climb herself?

Suddenly my attention was drawn again to the pulley beam. It projected out over the alley to the rear of the building, a little way down from the place where the balcony had been. The beam was directly over the place where I had noticed a pile of ash or sand in the alley below, moments before I had spotted Polly Brown's body dangling from the rope.

In an instant, I realised how the fiend might have accomplished his gruesome task, though if I lived to be a hundred, I should never understand why.

My mind working at a fever pitch, I imagined the scene as it must have been two nights before. Here the killer had crouched, peering down into the alley behind the Opera House and waiting for a likely victim to happen along. A girl, young and slim, walking alone. Miss Brown would have turned the corner and started down the narrow pathway, perhaps lost, perhaps thinking to take a short-cut. The fiend above had judged his moment and then leapt from the rooftop, gripping a rope threaded through the double pulley system, his descent slowed by a sandbag such as are used as counter-weights in theatres, to control the lowering of heavy painted back-drops.

Alighting beside his victim, the villain must then have ensnared her with a hook or noose – I shuddered to recall my own near-hanging at Newgate – and then stepped away, his own weight free of the rope. The sandbag plummets, dragging the terrified girl skywards. Perhaps the assassin breaks its fall when it reaches him upon the ground. He swarms up the rope, swings to the rooftop, then hauls his choking prey to him, cutting the rope and allowing the sandbag to fall the remaining distance, where it splits open against the cobbles beneath. The rest was clear enough.

This had been an act of physical daring and twisted imagination that surpassed all sanity, and yet as Lea had surmised, it was also the product of a meticulously tactical mind. I could see no reason to go to such extraordinary lengths unless Ned's intuition had been correct. The killer was a sadist and a narcissist; the challenge of accomplishing the task, of testing himself against the odds and displaying his victories, was itself the point.

I was no closer to finding the murderer, but I had gained insight into his methods and character; for the present, that would have to do.

Chapter 21

On my way back across the roof-scape, heading for the nearest hotel, I was hailed by a whistle that I recognised as being a salute of the Shivering Jemmies. I came to a stop perched upon the gable and waited a short while, and then down slid two of them; their leader, the girl Jegane, and a young boy. Jegane addressed me first.

"Please, Mr. Jack, but can you 'elp us?"

"Perhaps I can. What is the problem?"

"This 'ere is Tegim. 'is brother Charlie is apprenticed to Gamfield the Sweep - so was Tegim before 'e came to us - an' now 'e fears for Charlie's life." As she talked, Jegane expertly rolled a short, thick cigarette wrapped in newspaper. The boy stayed silent but nodded vigourously.

"This Gamfield, is he the man you spoke of when last we met? The one who would kill you if he sees you? I must know more about him."

"No, and it's ill luck to speak of that one, Jack - but Gamfield's bad enough all the same. 'e likes 'em young, does Gamfield." At this, Tegim looked away and down at the shingles, and I took her meaning well enough. I had heard tales of the horrific ill-treatment dealt out by some chimney-sweeps to their "apprentices", who were often little more than slaves.

Going by their manner, I was inclined to believe Jegane's blunt report; there was the chance that she was exaggerating for effect, but it could not hurt to make stronger allies of the Shivering Jemmies, and the lot of a cruel chimneysweep was little enough to me. Most important, though, was to learn more about this other violent man of the rooftops.

"I'll help you, then." The boy looked up sharply, his expression eager, and I saw no guile in his eyes, merely hope; it was enough for me.

"Thank you, Sir. Me bruvver don't deserve that life, e's only eight."

"I understand. How do you mean to rescue him?"

Jegane spoke again, around the smouldering stub of her cigarette;

"We know that Charlie will be up the main chimbly of the Kellogg house in Shaftesbury Avenue, around noon, two days 'ence. We'll pass word to 'im that 'es to make for the roof, but Gamfield will be up after 'im in a flash …"

"… and I shall be there to ensure that Charlie makes his escape," I finished.

"If you would, Mr. Jack. Gamfield's a terror to anyone smaller, but I reckon you'd be more'n enough to see 'im off. We'll look after Charlie once 'es away."

"Very well, then. I shall meet you on the Kellogg roof on Wednesday morning, and we shall give Mr. Gamfield something to think about."

"Thank you, Jack!" Tegim had brightened, and waved back at me as the two children made off across one of their balance planks, the feathers sewn into their burlap capes fluttering a little in the breeze, and then across the roofs towards their Belfry. As I watched them depart I was given pause to reflect again upon the extraordinary lives that passed above and beyond the attention of most Londoners.

Chapter 22

Inspector Lea,

have your men scale the Opera House in Dean Street, and search the rooftop; search also in the alleyway behind the theatre and I am sure that you shall deduce the methods used by the killer of Polly Brown. I suspect that he may have some experience with the rigging of ropes and counter-weights, perhaps as part of the theatre trade, or on board ship.

You have no cause to believe me, but for what ever it is worth, know that I played no part in this girl's death other than to try to prevent it. Tragically, I failed in that effort. I shall do what I can to atone for that failure and bring her assailant to justice, as I know you shall.

Should you wish to contact me, you may do so by means of a classified advertisement in the "Times". I hope that we can help each other.

With my sincerest regards to you, Sir,

I remain –

"Spring Heeled Jack"

I posted this letter en route to visiting Ned, who had lost no time in volunteering his services to one of the Anti-Garroting groups. He had been issued with a spiked steel collar, a bizarrely fashionable item intended to dissuade this particularly prevalent form of assault, and a sturdy, somewhat flexible cosh of the type known as a "life preserver", a spar of whalebone wrapped in leather and tipped with a lead ball. Thus armed and armoured, Ned's group patrolled the streets and public parks of Camden Town for several hours each night before repairing to one of the local taverns.

The presence of vigilante societies upon the streets was uneasily tolerated by the Metropolitan Police, who appreciated the extra deterrence but feared that the Societies, lacking professional training and judgement, would ultimately cause more problems that they would solve. And so it seemed to be, according to Ned's report.

"'Tis largely a waste of time, Sir," he sighed. "They're good-'earted lads in my crew but they don't know their arses from their elbows, most of 'em. And there's plenty of talk about what the other crews get up to. I 'eard that the South Bank Society baled up some poor bugger just because he was wearin' white, and one o' them remembered that from the Times article about the Alsop girl. They gave 'im a sound thrashing and all."

I explained my discoveries and deductions of the previous night, and Ned shook his head in disgust tinged with wonderment.

"So what we 'ave is a madman with both brawn and brains. What d'ye suggest, Cap'n?"

"I've sent an anonymous letter to Inspector Lea, pointing him towards the Opera House rooftop. I hope that it reaches him and that he heeds it, but he must be swamped with crank messages of all sorts. Beyond that, I shall continue to patrol the city by night, and 'Jack Haining' shall maintain appearances when the Wellingtonians meet next week. I fear that we are playing a waiting game, my friend."

Sadly, we would not have to wait very long.

Chapter 23

The next night I returned to the roofs, seeking any further sign of the mysterious assassin. I found none and was making my way back to the nearest hotel, more than a mite frustrated, when I spotted a commotion on the outskirts of Covent Garden. A few leaps brought me close enough to be able to see that an elderly pie-vendor's cart had been overturned by a pack of roughs. Normally I would be inclined to let this sort of petty street crime go, but that evening I was in a fighting mood.

As the rascals rounded upon the hapless old man and prepared to lay in their boots, I dropped down amongst them in a cloud of scarlet smoke. At this turn they scattered in some disorder.

One of the miscreants, presumably the leader, fancied himself a dab hand with the cudgel and put up some spirited resistance with his loaded cane. He batted away as if he were at Lord's Field; these blows I deflected handily with my greaves and then boxed both his ears for him with tight, left and right rounding hits, whereupon he too fled the scene.

The old pie-man pulled himself up from the gutter and bawled, "The rapscallion has me takings! Oh, stop him, do!" And in this, also, I found myself glad to oblige, springing off down the road after the ragged-arsed rascal and overtaking him just before he disappeared into the maze of dank alleys around Soho. The streets were still quite busy and this pursuit attracted no small amount of interest, with shouts and alarums, some folk rushing up to see Spring Heeled Jack in action, and others fleeing in terror.

In any case, I made quick work of the rough, slinging him into a nearby stile and then shooting ether into his face until he became silly and sat down with a thump, whereupon a young constable broke through the ring of onlookers and, taking stock of the situation with commendable speed, clapped the dazed ruffian in darbies.

"Nicely done," I said, "and if you care to search his pockets, you shall find the stolen night's takings of yonder pie-man."

"Hold, there!" responded the Peeler, "for you are a wanted … er … you're bound by law to … that's to say …"

Perhaps my celebrity had the better of him, but at this I confess that I lost interest and hopped over his head and away, with the moustachioed and becloaked Peeler gathering himself and giving chase, twirling his rattle for all he was worth. All of this was to the great amusement of the crowd, who evidently considered turnabout to be both fair play and dashed good sport.

Sadly for the young constable, he was brought up short by a tall iron gate, which had bothered the Spring Heeled Jack for not one moment. In high spirits after the pursuit, I called back to him, quoting a line I recalled from the newspapers: "The day is yours – leave the night to me!"

This incident was witnessed by a sketch artist whose (rather good) picture appeared in the Times a few days later, causing the hapless lawman no end of embarrassment, I am sure.

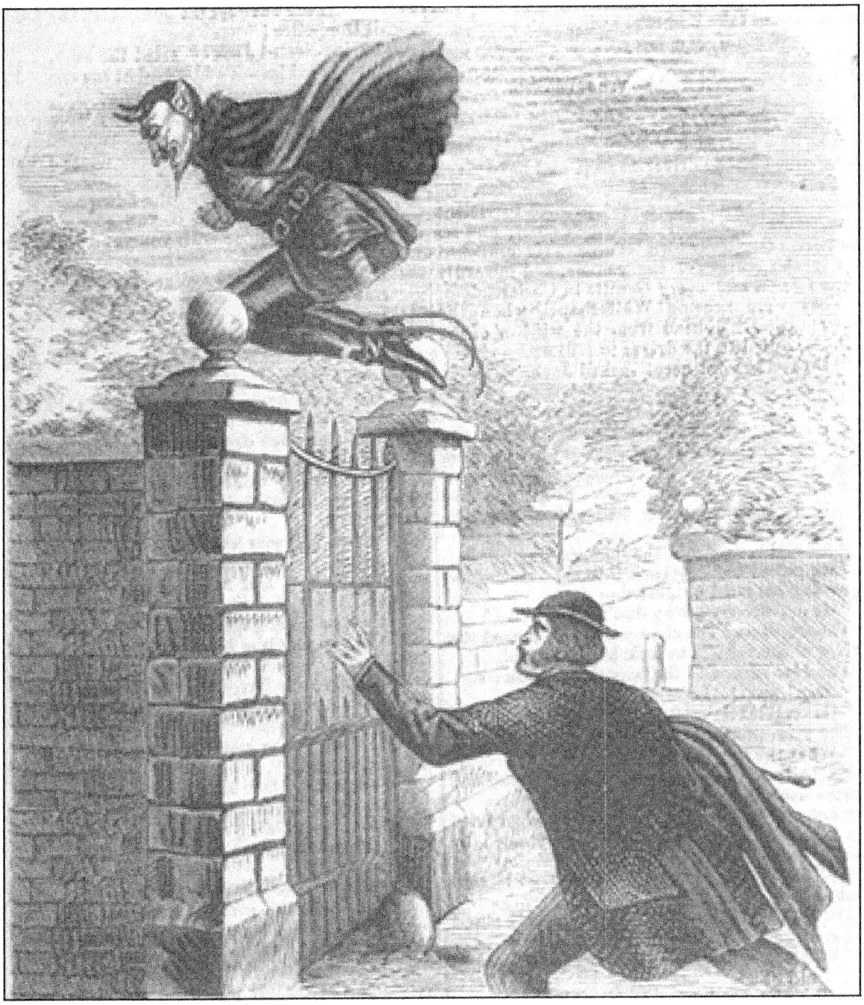

Chapter 24

On Wednesday morning, I rendezvoused with Jegane, Tegim and two other Jemmies, a boy and a girl, at our appointed spot, high atop the Kellogg mansion in Shaftesbury Avenue. It was dim and foggy and the children passed the time huddled together for warmth, sharing smoke from their newspaper cigarettes and short clay pipes and chatting amongst themselves in their strange cant. At one point they even deigned to address me in ordinary English, asking me to settle a dispute about marksmanship with their catapults; the Jemmies took turns shooting at a weathervane on the neighbouring roof and I adjudged Jegane's aim to be the truest, which was accepted with equanimity.

I was bemused by their attitude towards me, which seemed to combine a grudging respect and the sort of affection that an ordinary child might display towards a prize-winning pet dog or pony.

Finally, in the midst of an extraordinarily thick cloud of fog that dampened sound and light as well as all of us, a grimy little face popped out of the main stack.

"Charlie! Charlie, over 'ere!" whispered Tegim anxiously.

Charlie peered through the murk and his eyes went wide with fear. I realised at that moment that the Jemmies had neglected to mention my part in the escape plan to him.

"It's the Devil!", Charlie sputtered. "It's Springle Jack!"

"It's all right, you daft sod – 'es with us!" Tegim insisted.

"What d'you mean, 'es with you?! 'E's the bleedin' Devil!"

"Shut up and trust me," Tegim rasped. "I'm yer brother an' I'm tellin' you, 'es on our side. Now get your arse out of there."

"I can't, Gamfield's got me on a rope!"
This was unexpected. I did not want to speak – the youngster was so skittish I feared that he might decide that Gamfield was the lesser of two evils. Fortunately, Jegane spoke for me:

"Look you, just climb out and be quick about it – we'll sort the rest for you." At this encouragement, young Charlie did emerge from the flue. Immediately, we all heard the curses of Gamfield, both muffled and echoing as chimneys are wont to render speech.

"By Gawd, boy, what're you playin' at, eh? I'll 'ave yer, I swear it … don't you make me climb up there …"

"'ow far down is 'e?" Jegane asked of Charlie.

"Only one story …" the boy began, when suddenly the rope about his waist jerked taut and he flew backwards, coming up against the stack with a vicious bump. The man below evidently had his full weight to the rope and was climbing up towards us.

As one, the Jemmies and I sprang forward and gripped the rope to relieve the pressure upon poor Charlie, who looked to be in danger of being cut in half.

"On three!" I cried, and upon that count we all heaved, pulling Charlie clear of the stack and hauling the cursing Gamfield up rather faster than he had expected to travel. The sweep's frog-like, blackened face popped out of the flue in a puff of soot.

At this, I had my moment; poised upon a chimney pot and spreading my cape dramatically, I roared, "This boy is under my protection! Trouble him again, and Spring Heeled Jack shall steal your breath away!" I followed this with a burst of maniacal laughter fit to startle Beelzebub himself.

Mr. Gamfield's comeuppance, courtesy of
Spring Heeled Jack.

Gamfield, apoplectic with fear, emitted a croaking moan and froze in place; at that instant, the Jemmies cut the rope and he vanished downwards again in a series of increasingly muffled thumps.

At this turn, the Jemmies broke into exulting whoops – I recalled that many of them had escaped from the cruel life of the apprentice sweep – and even the taciturn Jegane was grinning broadly beneath her permanent mask of soot.

"Mr. Jack, Mr. Jack, we did it!" Tegim helped Charlie to remove the rope and then, with a rather admirable bravado, tossed it down the chimney after Gamfield.

"We did indeed – I think that you may have heard the last of him, for some time at least."

While the others excitedly recalled their own parts in the adventure, Jegane approached me with a serious cast to her features.

"We owe you now, Jack," she said. "Name the favour, it's yours if we can pull it off."

I could see by the look in her eyes that the girl took such matters to heart, and in fact the Jemmies did have something that I needed.

"All right, Jegane. I would like you to tell me all you know of the other rooftop man – the one who hurts your friends. I understand that you believe that it is bad luck to speak of him, but I must ask you to take that chance. Does that sit squarely with you?"

"A deal," she replied, and we shook upon it.

"He's called the Gargoyle", Jegane began somberly, forking her fingers as if to ward off malign influence. "He killed Megary and Tegom and some Snakesmen from across the river. And he's killed groundlings."

"Who is this Gargoyle?"

"I don't know if he has another name. He's like you. He's a man who looks like the Devil, and he jumps. He likes to kill us."

Then young Charlie spoke, tremblingly:

"I f-fink 'es a ugly stone beast, Mr. Jack. We sees 'em, on the buildings, we d-do - the gargoyles, I mean. I fink e's one of them, only he can move when he likes."

The boy shuddered and Jegane put a comforting arm around his shoulders.

The other Jemmies joined in. Tegim reckoned that the villain had been a groundling once, a sailor who had mastered the rigging of tall ship masts and who he had fled to the roofs to escape the law. He was contradicted by the girl Kegatie, who asserted that the Gargoyle had been a thief "like us, when he was small" and that he had always lived on the rooftops.

There followed a fierce debate in rapid Jemmie cant, after which Jegane told me that she thought they were both right, in parts; the Gargoyle had been a thief, then a sailor, and he had lived on the roofs as long as any of them could recall.

Then she told me that the Gargoyle had drowned one of their friends, a girl named Megary, by throwing her into a sewer ditch. A Snakesmen boy from the roofs of the South Bank had simply been slung into the street from six stories when he had the misfortune of getting in the Gargoyle's way.

"We all hates 'im, Jack - the Kestrel 'as a bounty on 'is 'ead, but few could beat 'im and none is of a mind to try," Jegane said.

I asked her who this "Kestrel" might be.

"She's the queen of the River Rats. She wears a mask, like you, but you'd never catch 'er up 'ere on the roofs. Best pirate on the Thames, though, and a friend to us all."

I made a mental note to quiz Ned on this masked pirate queen.

The Jemmies did not know of the murder at the Opera House but they obviously lived in mortal dread of this Gargoyle – the Bogeyman of the rooftop children. No wonder that they had been afraid when first they saw me.

Finally, Jegane stepped boldly forward and asked:

"If you find where the Gargoyle is, will you kill him?"

"If I have to, I will kill him."

"That's good," the girl replied, and then she and her friends departed my company.

Chapter 25

Ned Burrage often asked after the welfare of the Shivering Jemmies and was pleased to hear my account of Gamfield's comeuppance at their hands, with some minor assistance from the Spring Heeled Jack. He'd heard no tell of the Gargoyle but confirmed what the Jemmies had said about the Kestrel. Ned suspected that, like himself, she was a descendant of one of the Scarecrow's night riders, making her own mark in smuggling and piracy.

"An ally, perhaps, for Spring Heeled Jack, if she is a friend to the Jemmies and their kind, and an enemy both to this Gargoyle and to the river police?" I asked.

"P'rhaps so," Ned replied, but doubtfully. "I can put a word about on 'is behalf, if ye like, Sir."

"I'd be obliged, old fellow."

Ned's crew of Anti-Garroters had recently shifted their attentions back to the streets about Soho; I sensed that the Sergeant, quite realistically, hoped more to keep the young bucks out of serious trouble than to actually come across our adversary in the act.

During our daylight waking hours, we ascertained that the swinish Roland was maintaining his usual rounds of the city, and had taken to betting on boxing matches, ingratiating himself with that class of sporting men known as "the Fancy". One morning he and his bully-boys actually hailed Ned's cab, and their talk was all of the new rules that had been proposed for gloved fighting, named for the Marquis of Queensberry, and of the pugilist Jem Mace, upon whom Roland had apparently wagered a staggering sum of my money. However, my cousin's behavior as a wealthy man-about-town offered no hint as to any impropriety that I might use as blackmail against him.

Over the next several days "Jack Haining" settled in to his new part-time role as broadsheet editor. Thankfully, nothing more had been heard of the Rooftop Assassin, as he became dubbed by those papers who cared to distinguish between that maniac and Spring Heeled Jack. I quickly developed a good working relationship with Charles

Lea and on several occasions chanced to meet again his charming sister.

In quick order, I learned that Catherine was a sculptress of some skill and renown, having studied in Florence and in Rome. Her works had been exhibited in several of the larger London galleries. She was also engaged as an art critic for the Sporting and Dramatic News and, though I knew precious little of that worthy sphere, her articles clearly demonstrated both a keen wit and professional's eye for quality.

Her self-appointed role with regards to her brother's project of the Wellingtonian Gazette was not precisely defined, though I must confess that she was of great help to me as a sort of proof-reader, offering an outside eye and excellent advice. With hindsight, I am inclined to say that she simply took pity on my earnest but mediocre editorial abilities and decided to make use of her talents for the benefit of all concerned.

The first issue of the Gazette was a great success, launched with due ceremony at the Alfredian Club. After the fete, Charles and Catherine invited me out for a late supper. One thing led to another, as they do, and when it came time for us to bid good-night, I made a point of inquiring as to Catherine's availability the next day, suggesting that we might take a stroll together. To this proposal she readily agreed, and suggested that we meet for lunch at a restaurant in the Covent Garden area.

I regret that I was a trifle late to meet Catherine, but she graciously laughed away my tardiness – and her laughter was enchanting. So it was that we set out to enjoy the late morning bustle of London town.

Approaching the Garden, she drew my attention to an elaborate picture chalked upon the pavement. Here an anonymous screever, as pavement artists designated themselves, had created a pastel montage of the Spring Heeled Jack's escapades. In the centre was a fine portrayal of my mask, so true to life that the artist must have been drawing from memory; radiating outward were vignettes showing Jack bounding across the rooftops and a rather fanciful representation of the Guildford highway robbery, all exquisitely shaded and detailed.

"Oh, but this is marvellous work!" Catherine exclaimed.

"Yes, it's very clever," I replied. "Sadly ephemeral, though – come the next good rain, this will all be washed away."

"All the more reason to enjoy it while we can, then."

As I said, she was an enchanting woman.

We dropped some coppers into the artist's hat and started to move away. A pair of young Street Arabs then began to hop back and forth over the screeving, chanting thus:

"I come from Pandemonium, if they lay me I'll go back
Meanwhile 'round the town I'll jump -
Spring Heeled Jack!"

Impressed and amused both by the screeving and, increasingly, by Catherine Lea, I offered her my arm and we continued down the street towards the Covent Garden Market. Large, boisterous crowds had gathered at different points around the square and I was reminded of the mob that had appeared when Spring Heeled Jack had dealt to a young ruffian in that very area, some weeks past. For a moment I worried that our stroll was to be spoiled by street fighting, but as we drew closer, I realised that this was far off the mark; these crowds were gathered in innocent fun, to watch the antics of the jugglers and buskers.

Arm in arm, we paused to admire the skill and ingenuity of these street performers. Here there was a Punch and Judy man, hidden inside his canvas stage, who sent his audience of young children and their nannies into peals of near-hysterical laughter. As we watched, a little dog puppet sprang out from a concealed flap in the side of the canopy and barked like mad, provoking a chorus of gleeful shrieks; and then a puppet Spring Heeled Jack popped up and sparred with Mr. Punch. Jack lost that fight, of course.

Across the square a juggler balanced a spinning paper parasol upon his nose, and next to him, a troupe of hose-clad acrobats were setting up their ladders, poles and barrels. Everywhere was fun and laughter and I stole a glance at Catherine, who was clearly charmed by the spectacle.

I could not help but imagine the two of us visiting there again, perhaps in the not-distant future ... but then I caught myself. "Jack Haining", the new editor of the Wellingtonian Gazette, was no less a masquerade than was the Spring Heeled Jack himself. I was deceiving Catherine at that very moment, and myself, no less, with imaginings of romance ...

Chapter 26

Another Rooftop Murder!

Has "Spring Heeled Jack" Claimed his Second Victim?

The mutilated body of Miss Alice Masterson, who had been aged seventeen years, was sighted by hundreds of early-morning commuters making their way in to the City of London this morning. Her corpse dangled head-first from the lightning-rod atop the domed clock-tower of the Royal Exchange building at an estimated height of some one hundred and seventy feet.

Horrified onlookers could but watch helplessly as workers scrambled up hastily-erected ladders and made their perilous way to the girl, but this operation took nearly an hour to complete safely and she was dead by the time she had been brought down.

Miss Masterson was last seen by her mother, Mrs. Elva Masterson, at their home in nearby Threadneedle Street, on Friday night. Her window and the front door of the house are reported to have been locked from the inside throughout the night and were so when Miss Masterson's parents discovered that she was missing from her bed. There was no sign of a struggle in the girl's bedroom.

The Metropolitan Police under the command of Inspector Charles Lea have cordoned off the sites and are due to hold a conference for the press on Monday morning. A source close to Inspector Lea was able to confirm that the police are treating this case as another in the string of Spring Heeled Jack or "rooftop assassin" assaults and murders that have lately plagued London.

The very next Saturday, the newspapers trumpeted the headlines that all of London had been dreading. The circumstances of this new outrage were so improbable that Ned and I had to read the article several times to take it all in. Stunned by this, I quickly turned to the Classifieds and read –

S.H.J.; I share your hope. 9 of the clock, Monday evening atop the Opera House. C.L.

"It's bound to be a trap, Cap'n," Ned exclaimed. "For all that Lea's said, Spring Heeled Jack must at least be worth bringing in for questioning."

"I have no choice but to trust him," I replied. "The roof of the Opera House is easily scanned for treachery."

"The man is no fool. He'll be armed, Sir, and not alone, and yer harness is no' sure proof against bullets."

"I'll be careful, Ned."

And so I was, at a quarter of nine that Monday night, returned again to Soho, surveying the Opera House rooftop and those surrounding with a keen eye. A part of me expected Peelers lurking behind every smokestack. That they were not – that, in fact, I beheld only Inspector Lea himself, standing with his back to me and gazing out over the roofscape much as I had a week before – spoke volumes for the fellow's self-confidence. He had gained the roof via a long bamboo ladder from the fire escape, and I would need to keep an eye on that, against the emergence of a stealthy constable or three.

With a mighty bound I propelled myself across the final twenty-foot gap and then, with another, launched myself up to land upon one of the chimneys behind him, achieving such a height that I might still have a chance to escape in two jumps, should Ned's warning prove to be prophetic.

"Inspector!"

He raised his arms away from his sides and turned slowly towards me, his expression changing commendably little when he beheld a seven-foot tall demon perched upon a chimney-pot, some five yards away.

"I will not move from this spot, if you will promise not to move from yours," he called out.

"Agreed."

"*Quid pro quo*, Sir – those are my terms." Lea looked hard at me and I knew that he was memorising every detail of my appearance.

"I accept, Sir."

"Firstly – I trust that you did attempt to rescue Polly Brown after the word of my constable who helped to bring her down. Do you have any further information pertaining to her death?"

"Nothing. I happened upon the scene and did what I could, then returned to this spot a day later and deduced how she had been abducted from the alley."

"Very well. Ask your question."

"What were the circumstances of Miss Masterson's abduction?"

"We are not certain that she was abducted, but if so, we believe that the kidnapper entered her bedroom and spirited her away via the chimney flue. Her night-dress was in shreds – as was her body, come to that - and both were stained with soot. Lesions about her wrists suggest that she had been bound at some point, though her hands were free when she was hung from the Tower."

Lea stood as if to attention, but with arms spread and open palms turned towards me. I glanced over towards the fire-escape, but saw no movement there and he continued:

"My next question: are you the man responsible for the attacks against Sir Roland Ashton's men and the theft of his rent-money?"

"I am. Do you have any suspects in the Masterson and Brown murders?"

"We believe that the murderer is the same man who attacked two other girls in London over recent weeks. We have had a suspect in custody since Friday, but the Masterson case appears to exonerate him. Otherwise, I have suspicions, but no firm leads. Where were you at twelve o'clock on the night of Friday last?"

"I believe that I was patrolling the rooftops of the South Bank area."

"You were spotted there by several vigilantes and members of the public and by two of our officers, co-incident with the time that Miss Masterson must have met her fate. I doubt that even you could leap back and forth across the Thames, so I suppose that will serve as an alibi."

Still no movement from the fire-escape.

"My turn, Inspector. How do you surmise the killer secured Miss Masterson's body to the clock tower?"

"If you're asking how the deuce he got her up there, I was hoping that you would have some idea. I have not had time yet to examine the scene myself."

Lea seemed to sigh.

"I have no further questions for you," he continued, "but for what it's worth, I believe that there are two rooftop-leaping madmen on the loose in London and that you're not the one I'm looking for."

I was about to reply when Lea looked sharply down to my left and his expression instantly changed. He made to move his right hand and then there was a snap and a thud and Lea's head jerked. He spun about like a drunken dancer, staggering back and toppling toward the edge of the roof. I sprang towards him and barely managed to catch hold of his belt as he fell.

Thankful for my conditioning, I hauled him to safety. Blood was streaming from a wound over his right eye. I supported him for a moment, but he quickly shook me off and drew a pistol from his pocket.

"Lea, what happened?"

"Over there!" the Inspector gestured with the muzzle of his pistol and I thought for a moment that this was some bizarre ruse, that he meant to capture me; my own hand crept towards the flash-trigger in my belt. But no, even as he swept the flowing blood away from his eyes with his free hand, his gaze was still directed towards the stack from whence I had leaped.

"What was it, man? What did you see?"

Lea's eyes rolled and he faltered; I gripped his elbow to support him.

"There ... in the shadow ..."

I strained my eyes into the dark and could barely make out a pale figure lurking next to the chimney-stack. Next we heard a ringing, sardonic voice:

"There are two of us, indeed; and London is only big enough for one!"

Lea wiped blood from his eyes and seemed to rally.

"You'll not escape," he called. "I have men all around!"

"Yes, but they are earth-bound. It was Richard Steele who said: 'What nonsense is all the hurry of this world to those who are above it!' "

I could be upon the man in a single leap, but he held an unknown weapon and Lea was in a bad way. I held my ground and tensed to spring at a moment's notice.

"I have only this to say to you, gentlemen," the apparition continued. "The rooftops of London are mine alone, and I shall take what I will of the groundling girls. This city is my canvas, and my colour is red. Cross me at your mortal peril!"

At this, Lea fired into the space the mysterious assailant had occupied, but he was gone, slipped around the corner of the chimney-stack and out of our sight.

"Go! You take the left!" The Inspector ran in a stumbling crouch, his left hand clasping a handkerchief to his bleeding forehead, aiming to cut the man off; I sprang to the left of the chimney and whirled about the corner, gauntlets raised and ready to fight. But Lea and I came up face to face - the man had vanished!

Wheeling about and peering into the gloom, we saw a pale form leap from the far side of the rooftop, trailing a rope behind, and an instant later there came the crash of glass.

"Damn it to Hell!" Lea raced to the edge of the building and called out:

"All men below, this is Inspector Lea! The villain has escaped into the Opera House! Let no-one out!"

He turned back to me and faltered again, collapsing against the rough tiles. His eyes rolled deliriously and then closed. The wound was still bleeding freely, but as far as I could make out it was not too deep and I hoped that he was merely concussed. I pressed his handkerchief against the flow until I was distracted by the sounds of men running across the roof towards us.

"You there! Step away from him!"

I knew that the Peelers were in no mood to listen to my explanations and that they would see to the Inspector. I stood up, waited until they were close enough, and then closed my eyes and flicked the flash-trigger at my belt. The magnesium panel on my chest flared like summer lightning, the truncheon-wielding constable recoiled, dazzled, and I sprang high over his head and away.

I dropped in to the crypt and changed my clothes for those of Jack Haining, then made my way back to the Charing Cross Hotel. In my room, I turned the night's events over in my mind. How had the villain known of my meeting with Lea upon the roof? Either he had come across the Inspector's message to me in the Times by chance and had deciphered it, or he had a source within the Police who had tipped him off; or perhaps he had been following Lea or myself. The lattermost option was easily the worst for me, for it suggested that the villain might somehow have discovered my secrets. It took some time before I could sleep that night.

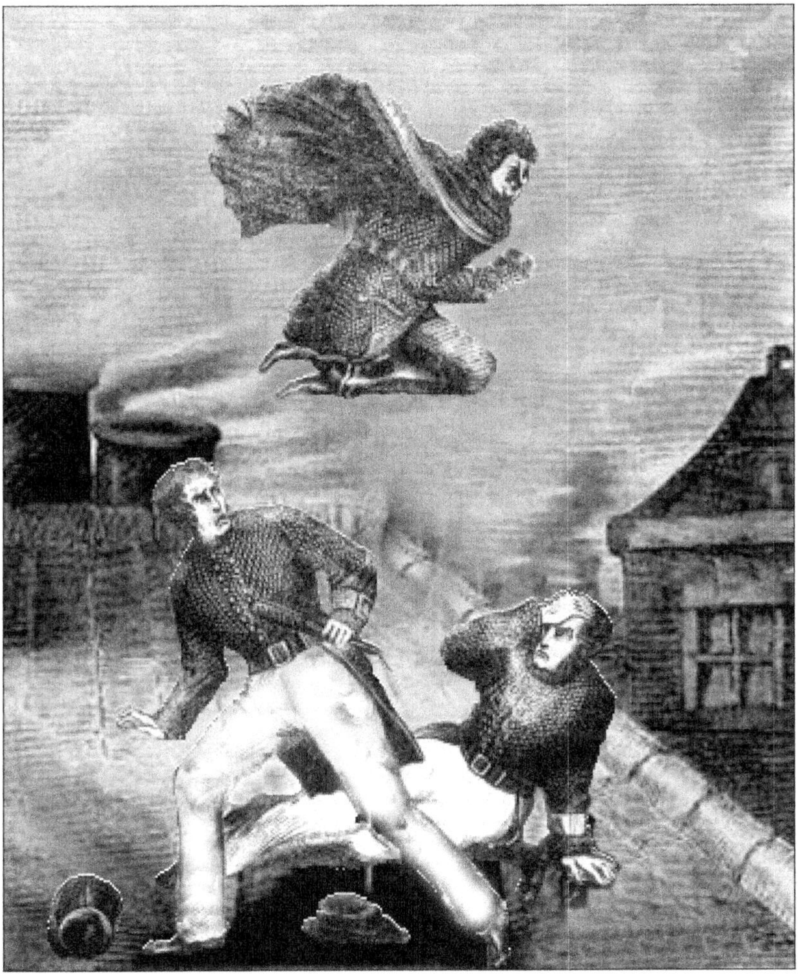

Chapter 27

The next afternoon, it being my feline habit to spend most nights prowling the roofs and then to sleep until mid-day, I opened my bedroom door as usual to find my copy of the Times and my breakfast of honey toast and milky mint tea awaiting me. I have never been able to abide large breakfasts.

I snatched up the newspaper and scanned through it quickly, alert to any mention of Lea's condition. On the third page it was mentioned that my old commanding officer, Colonel Manfred, would soon be visiting London; I felt a sharp pang, for the man had been like a second father to me, and the news of Jack Ashton's supposed treachery and death by hanging must have wounded him to the core.

The Classifieds were bereft of any messages from Lea, but – finally! - a paragraph buried in the middle of the paper noted that the Inspector had been injured in the line of duty the previous evening and would not be able to deliver the promised press conference until he had recovered. Evidently, the specific nature and cause of his injury had not been disclosed to the journalist; and apparently, going by the lack of any reports to the contrary, the villain had made his escape from within the Opera House. Once inside, of course, he would have had his pick of windows - curse the scoundrel's eyes, whoever he was!

I could do nothing but hope that Charles Lea would be well. He had impressed me as the best sort of man to have on one's side in a scrap, and in this he was spiritual kin to my boon companion, Ned.

I washed and dressed quickly, then left the hotel and made my way through a bright and crisp London afternoon to the site where Alice Masterson's body had been recovered, the imposing edifice of the Royal Exchange Tower. The police cordons were gone and the massive Exchange courtyard was even busier than usual; many spectators, I was sure, being drawn to the spot out of morbid curiosity. Innumerable merchants and tradesmen had set up their stalls and business was obviously booming.

Some twenty feet above, the courtyard was criss-crossed with a veritable spider's web of ropes and cords, from which hung all manner of colourful ribbons, flags and other bunting. It would have been a cheery scene except for the fading russet stain that spread down from the spire of the clock tower, to which many a sad and furtive glance was cast.

The Tower was the best part of two hundred feet in height, three tiers of pale stonework dripping with ornate cornices and bas-relief artwork depicting Classical images of industry. The great brass face of the clock rested just above the base of the second tier. Above that rose the belfry, topped with its smooth stone dome, and from the summit thrust the lightning rod from which the girl had been hung. Access to the dome would have been, if not easy, then at least achievable via a system of ladders. Given the layered shape of the Tower and the lack of projecting beams, I could not see how the villain might have used his ropes and pulleys to haul his victim up from the roof below.

If Lea's theory was correct, the blackguard had descended into the girl's bedroom in Threadneedle Street via the chimney flue. The Times article had mentioned that there was no sign of a fight in the bedroom itself, yet somehow he had made off with her via the same route, transported her across the road to the Exchange and then dragged her up to the tower. As I had in Soho, I strained to picture the fiend actually carrying a struggling, or even insensible, girl such a distance and over so many obstacles without some witness raising an alarm, this being one of the busiest thoroughfares in the city, even late at night.

I approached one of the vendors, bought one of his pastries and introduced myself as writer Jack Shaw, then asked if he knew the address of the Masterson's home.

"Oh, number seventy-two, Threadneedle, Sir. It was an awful thing to 'appen, such a young girl from a good family and all. I saw them trying to get her down, I did. That whole face of the dome was stained red, you can still see some of it. Dreadful, dreadful business."

I agreed and thanked him, then was struck by another thought.

"Do you know, was there any sign of forced entry into the building below the tower?"

"Not that I know of, Sir. The police were 'ere and they asked the same, but none of the lads could find any broken latches or anything of that sort. Nor even any ladders about other than those they keep in the maintenance buildings, and they was locked up overnight. That's the odd thing, 'ow did 'e get the girl up onto the dome? It's been the talk of the market, and the Exchange too, I shouldn't wonder."

"Of course." I thought back to the pile of sand that had been my clue to unravelling the murderer's method in the Soho alley.

"So there was nothing else to be seen when you came in that morning? Nothing at ground level to suggest how she got up there?"

The man's brow furrowed.

"I don't think so, Sir. There was a couple of lads fixing up the flags above. They was in a bit of tangle, but they get that way sometimes when the wind picks up."

I glanced speculatively up again at the web-work of lines overhead and thanked the man, then made my way from the crowded courtyard out towards Threadneedle Street, where I quickly located the home in question. It was a very tall and stately building, with the Union Jack, now at mourning half-mast, waving from a flagpole on the roof. The Mastersons were obviously well-off, perhaps connected to the stock exchange, as were many families in this area.

I crossed the street again and moved some way down the road in an attempt to take in the whole picture. From within number seventy-two, up through the chimney to the roof; thence down the outside wall or the fire escape, across the thoroughfare where now I stood and then over the walls of the Exchange, across the courtyard and up to the Tower dome. How had he done it?

I recalled his taunts towards Lea and myself the night before – "groundlings", he had called the people of London, and he had quoted Steele to the effect that the bustle of street life was a matter of little concern to those "above". I confess that I, too, had felt that sensation of superiority, sailing over the rooftops, free to do as I would – fay ce que voudras ... it would be easy, all too easy, to allow that sensation to curdle into contempt for my fellow men.

Of a sudden, it occurred to me that my enemy would likely scorn to descend to the street at all during one of his mad capers. If what the Jemmies had told me was true, then most of the Gargoyle's previous murders had been opportunistic and enacted against other denizens of the roofscape. As Ned had surmised, the fiend's attacks upon the Alsop and Scales girls had the nature of practice, as if he were testing his mettle or experimenting with new methods. Then he had snatched Polly Brown from the street and whisked her up to the roofs.

And now ... now I was coming to believe that he regarded himself as a master craftsman of spectacular murder. With that thought, gazing again upon the scene, a possible method came to mind. It would have required enormous effort, daring and careful planning, but I knew that all of these were well within his capabilities.

I resolved then that Spring Heeled Jack should undertake a mission to gain and inspect the roof of the Masterson home.

Chapter 28

The bells of the Exchange Tower were tolling nine of the clock as I touched down upon the gently sloping gables of the benighted house. The Union Jack now hung at half-mast, unmoving on its pole, the brightly moonlit night being very still. Across the street I could make out the dark bulk of the Tower itself, silhouetted against the stars.

I made my way first to the chimney stack. It was of the closed type, but the light of my lantern revealed that the ventilation cap had recently been disturbed – removed, obviously, by the villain to clear the way for his evil deed. Typical of such stately homes, the flue was easily wide enough to admit a full-grown man.

I peered down through the grille but could see nothing but inky blackness within, the pitch dark seeming even to swallow lantern-light after a few feet. I tried not to imagine the terror of poor Alice Masterson as she had been dragged up through this soot-stinking tunnel, and failing in that effort, felt a rage against her kidnapper and murderer that turned my very bowels to ice. The villain would pay dearly if I had anything to do with the matter.

I had theorised that he must have used some mechanical contrivance to accomplish this phase of his "operation", and in studying the base of the flag-pole I noticed that two rings of the weathered white paint had been worn away, exposing the wood beneath. My suspicion of that afternoon was that he had used some form of windlass, such as would be employed to raise the sails on a tall ship, and if he had, then the flag-pole would have made a fine anchor for the device. On closer inspection, the paint of the higher of the two rings was most worn away on the opposite side of the flagpole from the chimney, whilst the lower ring showed most wear on the side opposite the Tower across the street.

I stepped back and concentrated on the scene as it might have played out three nights before. Skulking upon the roof and listening down through the flue, the assassin had picked his moment carefully, giving Miss Masterson time to fall asleep before lowering his rope and descending into her room. Quickly overcoming the girl in her bed, perhaps stunning her with ether, he would have bound and probably gagged her before carrying her to the fireplace and securing her to the rope. Then, after climbing back up the flue, it would have been an easy matter to haul her up to the roof. Again, I was put in mind of a spider wrapping its prey.

Now I turned to face the dark bulk of the Tower across the street, imagining a second rope, threaded through a pulley system and drawn taut between the Masterson's flag-pole and the lightning rod atop the dome. Against the moonless night sky and beyond the glare of the gas-lamps, it would have been invisible to any passers-by at street level.

The angle up to the top of the dome was quite steep, I guessed close to forty degrees, and the distance across the void was considerable. I pictured the girl tied into some form of bosun's chair. The task of winching the chair from here to there might have taken half an hour and, even with the assistance of the pulleys, would have required extraordinary strength and endurance. Once he had her atop the dome, though, the Assassin would have had all the time he required.

Then, the escape; I imagined the villain sailing in his bosun's chair back down to the rooftop where I now stood; with the rope at that angle, the flight across the wide boulevard would have taken mere seconds. No, that would have left the other end of his rope attached to the tower ... but might he have lit a timed fuse attached to that end of the rope, a moment before he used it to effect his flight? It would have been an insane risk, but not one that I would put past this man.

From thence, the rope would have collapsed down onto the web of lines over the Exchange courtyard – I recalled the pastry vendor mentioning that the flags overhead had been disturbed - and into Threadneedle Street. The assassin could easily have gathered it back up to the Masterson's roof under the cover of darkness. I pictured him making his way down the fire escape at his leisure, or away across any of the neighbouring rooftops.

If the murder had played out as I had deduced, then it had been a diabolical crime, made more so by the extreme lengths to which the villain had gone in order to achieve his grisly spectacle. I resolved to get another message to Charles Lea immediately, in the hope that he might be able to use this information to bring the madman to bay, and so leaped from the edge of the Masterson roof to the next below.

It was on the third roof down that I suddenly came to a stop, hearing again the curious whispering that I had detected at Soho and elsewhere in the city. I stood still, balanced upon my springs and anticipating being hailed by the Jemmies, though this was far from their usual territory, but this was not to be. I recalled their talk of the Kestrel and of rival gangs, and repaired to the nearest hotel in a state of consternation.

As I prepared to take my rest, my thoughts returned to the Hellfire Club, to Roland, to the mysteries in which I had become embroiled. This was far indeed from the life that my dear father had planned for me.

Chapter 29

The next morning I was awoken by a knock on the door from faithful Ned.

"Hoping you slept well, Sir?"

"Odd dreams, old fellow."

"Aye, there's a bit o' that going about, I reckon. Must be the season."

I invited him in and we reviewed my investigations of the previous evening. I awaited his own report with some curiosity, for as a general rule we then reserved our face-to-face meetings for the Crypt. Our precaution was due to the notion that it might not do for Ned to be seen associating too closely with Messrs. Haining, Geoffreys or Shaw.

"First off, Sir, there's word back from the River Rats - that's the Kestrel's smuggling crew. She extends 'er regards to the Spring Heeled Jack and says there's money to be made on the Gargoyle's head."

"Indeed - Jegane also spoke of a bounty," I replied.

"And The Times reports that Inspector Lea has recovered," Ned continued. "'E's addressing the Wellingtonians again this evenin'."

"Good news. I feared for him."

"I was thinkin', Sir, if you're goin' to pursue this line – an' frankly, I still reckon it's an untoward risk gettin' so close to the Peelers – but the toffs at the Club might be able to offer a clue or two in the Hellfire boys' direction."

"The Alfredians are a conservative bunch, Ned – I can't credit them with anything so exotic as guising masks and pagan labyrinths."

"I'm not sayin' they're in on that game, Cap'n, but we've come up wi' naught else so far. All we know is that whoever the Hellfire Club may be, they're not usin' the caves at Medmenham Abbey. It couldn'ae hurt to poke around a bit here in London, ask your Clubmen what's what."

"You might well be right, at that. I'll visit the Club tonight for Lea's address, and make some discreet inquiries."

Ned grinned around his pipe, saluted and then bade me farewell and left to begin his cab rounds. I quickly drafted another note to Lea over breakfast in the dining room, recapping my investigations of the Masterson home and my speculations about the murderer's latest means. It was near noon by the time I posted the letter, leaving me some time to while away, and this I spent strolling through the East End theatre district.

In Drury Lane I spotted a playbill on the brick face of the Theatre Royal, announcing that George Conquest, the actor and acrobat whose Mephistophelian disguise had partially inspired my own, was now appearing in a drama entitled "Spring Heel'd Jack, or, the Felon's Wrongs". The bill bore a garish illustration of a truly chimeric figure, sporting fangs, bat-like wings and a great leonine mane of black hair, in the act of stuffing a Peeler head-first down a chimney-stack. I was, in equal parts, amused by the irony, appalled by the likeness, and impressed by the speed at which newspaper reports and street folk-lore had been turned into popular entertainment. I souvenired the bill and decided that I owed George Conquest a drink.

An hour before the Wellingtonians' meeting that night, writer "Jack Haining" again found himself in conversation with their Chairman. The effusive Frederick Barnes was delighted that I was investigating the history of London's "friendly societies" and gentlemen's clubs, and impressed that I had been civic-minded enough to want to support the efforts of the Wellingtonians as well. We sat down at the bar and it soon became apparent that, although Barnes was no scholar of the occult, he was a fount of knowledge on related matters.

Mr. Barnes spoke for some time as I took notes, detailing the origins of the Clubs in the practices of Medieval trade guilds and, more recently, literary societies and mutual aid fraternities. Eventually the

The playbill for "Spring Heel'd Jack, or, the Felon's Wrongs".

opportunity arose for me to question him specifically about the infamous Hellfire Club, and its potential survival or re-incarnation.

"As near as I know, Mr. Haining, the Hellfire lads were a pack of aristocratic Mohocks. I am certain that there is no Club now using that name in London, nor have I heard of it elsewhere, but perhaps you would also care to speak to Mr. Stevens? He has a long-standing interest in these affairs. Here, I shall introduce you."

Barnes led me towards the Club library, and hailed a fellow who was, as we entered, balancing rather perilously atop a short ladder in quest of a book upon a high shelf. He turned and I saw him to be a slender man of perhaps sixty years, with a head of grey hair and a full beard, spectacles upon his nose, the very picture of an antiquarian scholar.

"Henry Stevens, this is Jack Haining, a new Alfredian and a writer by trade. Mr. Haining is interested in the old Hellfire Club and I thought you might be able to help him."

"Oh, yes, of course," Stevens replied, climbing down from his perch and shaking my hand, upon which we all returned to the bar. I was mildly surprised to recognise his accent as American; somehow, one did not anticipate American scholars taking a great interest in the histories of British clubs.

I also thought it passing strange that a man of such staid mien should think it proper to discuss the Hellfire Club, with its debaucheries and mock-Satanism, but Stevens was evidently an open-minded fellow and a passionate antiquarian. Barnes ordered Scotch for the three of us, and our American colleague began to address his subject.

"Now, Mr. Haining, I take it that you already know the fundamentals, Sir Francis Dashwood and so-forth. Have you yet visited the old Abbey at Medmenham?"

"Yes, I was there several weeks ago."

"Fascinating place, sadly neglected these days. Of course, you know that the Hellfire Club disbanded some hundred years ago … ?"

"I do indeed, Sir - but would you think it possible that the Hellfire Club could have survived in secret, or perhaps have been reformed?" I asked him.

"I think that – well, certainly not impossible, but unlikely. Most secret societies are formed for a particular purpose, and comparatively few retain much mystery about them beyond their first generation."

As Stevens warmed to his subject I received the distinct impression that he might be a professor as well as a scholar, for I was reminded of attending tutorials during my carefree student days at Cambridge.

"Those that do," he continued, "are of a primarily political, especially revolutionary, or criminal nature. The standard pattern otherwise is to dissolve into a benign fraternal order or drinking club, or simply to disperse. The chances are better that some of the original members transported aspects of the Hellfire Club's rites to other Clubs, after the original group factionalised."

Dashwood himself, I recalled, had been affiliated with the Masons and had served as a secret agent for the Jacobite cause. This at least suggested an active, political dimension that would seem to have been a far cry from the debaucheries popularly associated with the Club of a hundred years ago. Increasingly, it sounded as if Abbot Holt's description of the modern Club had been accurate and honest. It could well have survived in secret for the past hundred years as a sort of shadow council, a political entity retaining some of the original Hellfire theatrics, which, I knew from my own experience, might also serve a tactical purpose.

We continued to chat for a while but it had become obvious that, as with the good people of High Wycombe, as far as my fellow Alfredians were concerned the Hellfire Club was nothing but a diverting historical footnote. Eventually Mr. Barnes was called away to prepare for the meeting of the Wellingtonian Society. Henry Stevens wished me luck and returned to his research in the library, and I followed Barnes into the oak-panelled meeting room, which was already near-full. I was relieved to note that Roland was not in attendance.

Charles stood behind the lectern, his temple bandaged, attended by Catherine and a young constable who was presently passing out the latest edition of the Wellingtonian Gazette. Charles and Catherine smiled at me as I entered and I offered an encouraging nod, then found an inconspicuous seat toward the back of the room.

Lea's address that night was typically professional, an accurate summation of the circumstances already reported in the Times.

As he spoke, though, I noted that Catherine seemed extremely concerned for him. At one point, the Inspector became uncharacteristically flustered and appeared to be unable to find his place in his notes, and she rose gracefully and indicated the point for him. This was worrisome to me, for despite the fact that Lea would surely be obliged to arrest me on the spot if he had any idea of my true identity, or that of the Surrey highwayman, Spring Heeled Jack, I admired and liked the man. I dreaded to think that the would-be assassin's missile should have caused him any permanent damage.

As Lea was coming to the end of his presentation, he thanked the Wellingtonians for their civic-mindedness and asked again that the group should sustain its efforts in lending a voice of reason and restraint to the city, particularly with regards the management of the Anti-Garroting Societies.

"Vigilante justice has its place on our streets, Gentlemen," he said. "Upon rare occasion, certain well-intentioned activities of an extra-legal nature can be of great help to the Police and to the people of London. However, I urge you to maintain your sober guidance of these Societies. As I am sure that you will all agree, the last thing we need is for all of this spirit and vigour to turn sour."

I had noted the presence of several reporters in the audience and confess that I could not help but hear this as a warning also to Spring Heeled Jack. Although Lea had not, of course, mentioned our encounter during his address, I wondered if it might also be worth checking the next day's Times Classifieds.

Chapter 30

There was, as it turned out, no further message from Lea via the newspapers, and I'd had no opportunity to speak with him after the meeting, so in the late afternoon of the following day I set out to visit him as Jack Haining, on the pretext of Wellingtonian Gazette business. In truth, I simply hoped to ascertain that he was not too badly hurt by the rooftop assailant's missile.

As neither were married, Charles and Catherine lived together in the home they had inherited from their parents, a handsome terrace house in Symons Street, just off Sloane Square.

Catherine answered me at the door and, once the formal pleasantries were offered and received, invited me into their parlour and set about fixing us a spot of tea.

"I do trust that Charles is not too sore?" I asked.

"He's resting now, on doctor's orders," she replied. "He tripped, you see, and gave his head a nasty crack upon the edge of the dining table."

Of course, I instantly forgave her the lie - Haining could hardly be permitted to know the true cause of Charles' injury.

"I'm sorry to hear it, Miss Lea," I offered.

"Oh, you really must learn to call me Catherine!"

"Catherine … and please call me Jack."

She smiled.

"Charles will appreciate your concern, Jack. He holds you in esteem."

"And I him."

I passed on my sheaf of notes towards an article for the next Wellingtonian Gazette, and we chatted some more on this and that, sipping our tea, until conversation turned toward Catherine's latest sculpture. I expressed a desire to see the work in progress and she demurred, but not much, and then we repaired to the small conservatory in their back garden, which served as her studio. Here were the benches where she worked in clay, modelling the creations that would, sometimes, later be cast in immortal metals.

"Can you guess, Jack?" she teased, indicating a form shrouded by a clay-spattered sheet. I confessed that I could not, and then she unveiled her work with a flourish, and I beheld a masterpiece in gleaming bronze; an owl with wings and talons outspread. I was taken aback by the artistry.

"I ... I'm sorry, Catherine, I do not mean to flatter, but this is extraordinary!"

I walked about the work, the better to appreciate the textured feathers, the suggestion of taut muscles bunched beneath, the marvellous sense of violent predation forever frozen in an instant.

"You are too kind ... but no, away, false modesty!" she laughed. "In candor, I'm very pleased with this piece and shall be sad to see it go."

"Where to?"

"The Zoological Society has commissioned a series inspired by the animals of Classical myth - a roe deer for Apollo, this owl for Athena and several others. They shall be arranged about the gardens, that visitors may come upon them unexpectedly."

"The owl of Minerva takes wing only when the shades of dusk do gather," I managed to quote.

"Hegel?" she asked.

"I believe so," I replied, and then suddenly she took my hand and kissed my cheek.

"You are sweet, Jack Haining," she said softly and solemnly, "and I'm pleased to know you."

At that moment, I confess that I flushed and looked away.

"Oh Jack, now I'm sorry - I was too bold ..." Catherine released my hand.

"No, please," I replied, "it is not that. In truth, it has been long since ... since anyone has shown me such regard. It has unmanned me, but ..."

I took her hand again, and we two stood close for some time, neither speaking, as the shades of dusk did gather about Minerva's owl.

Chapter 31

Much later that evening I was trailing Roland's coach, en route to one of Jem Mace's prize-fights on the outskirts of the city, when I was hailed by the now-familiar whistle of the rooftop children.

"Jack! We need you!"

It was Jegane and two of her urchin compatriots, all seemingly perturbed.

"I have other business this night, Jegane."

"It's h'urgent, it is! It's the Gargoyle! We know where he is, but you must come now!"

The coach was rounding a corner down below, but I decided to leave Roland to his boxing. "Where, girl?"

"Best if I show yer," Jegane replied. She ordered her friends away and then started to lead me across the roofscape towards Southwark. She had evidently made this trip many times before, as she negotiated the roofs with ease, scuttling up and down walls and vaulting obstacles as if born to it. Several times we paused while she manoeuvred planks into position from their hiding places, sliding them out to rest between the ledges of two neighbouring buildings. Jegane crossed these makeshift bridges as casually as if they were suspended mere inches above the ground.

We were moving steadily towards the Thames, a wide strip of inky blackness illuminated only by the occasional boat's lantern.

Eventually we arrived at the site of the Victoria Dock, which was being expanded at the time. This was the first London dock to be built for steam ships, and it was presently a maze of immense, half-completed ship-bays connected by an ascension of scaffolding towers, platforms and ladders rising some eighty feet into the dark sky. Jegane started to climb the towers, moving nimbly and apparently tirelessly from one tier to the next. Looking down, I could see moonlight reflected from deep pools of water between the artificial islands that supported the towers.

It must have been near midnight when Jegane stopped atop the highest tower at the edge of one of the bays, a platform bordered on one side by a large canvas sail. She lit one of her pungent newspaper cigarettes and then pointed with the glowing ember across the river and towards the landscape of wharves and warehouses that was Bermondsey.

"There, the tallest smokestack. That's the Grange Tannery. The Gargoyle's there, up on the roofs."

"Thank you."

Jegane drew hard, causing the tobacco to crackle, and winced a little at its bite. She looked me in the eye through the smoke, but only briefly.

"You see that lantern, Jack?"

She now pointed down toward the inky river, and I made out a pale light bobbing not too far away.

"That's the Kestrel's skiff. She'll take you across."

"I see it. Thank you, Jegane."

"All right, then," she replied. She began to move away, then paused and glanced back at me.

"If you can't kill him, then he will kill you."

I raised my hand in farewell as the girl scurried down into the darkness, and the I was suddenly struck by a tremendous impact from behind, sending me reeling towards the edge of the platform. I managed a pirouette and whirled about at the brink, knocked breathless.

"Good evening to you, Master Jack!"

There stood my nemesis, poised like a dancer, both arms wrapped about long ropes reaching up into the dark tangle of masts and poles above the platform, from whence he had swung. The girl had lured me into a trap!

The Gargoyle was an extraordinarily ugly man, with bulging eyes and a face that had obviously received some ancient trauma, for his nose was quite crushed flat against his cheekbones, and his forehead was heavily scarred and dented inwards. His evil leer displayed a set of missing teeth between sharp canines. His ears were also severely misshapen, bulbous and knotted, like those of a pugilist who has stayed far too long in the ring.

He wore a padded jerkin of pale oilskin, like a fencing-master's vest, with long coils of rope looped around his thick shoulders in the manner of bandoliers. His knees and elbows were wrapped in leather swathes. Bizarrely, he also wore a battered top hat pulled hard down about his gnarled ears. The canvas sail behind him flapped in a sudden breeze and the effect was that of some nightmarish pirate of yesteryear, come to visit rapine and pillage upon the city of London.

He called into the night:

"Well done, Jegane! Your package awaits you, as arranged, my dear."

"I'm sorry, Jack, I truly am!" came the girl's voice, now far below us. "I swear it, 'e gave me no choice!"

"The Shivering Jemmies have their uses, Jack," the horror continued, for all the world if we were strolling together along the Strand. "I took the liberty of absconding with one of Jegane's young comrades, a brave little mite recently escaped the sour lot of a sweep's apprentice. She and Mistress Kestrel will find him trussed up like a Christmas goose and hanging in a burlap sack off the side of Bermondsey Dock, not much the worse for his ordeal, so long as the tide has not yet risen too high." At this, the Gargoyle glanced speculatively at the black waters.

Charlie! I understood Jegane's treachery now; she had been coerced by a dire threat to the life of a helpless child. The Kestrel's motive was less clear.

"A fascinating lot, the rooftop urchins," the Gargoyle continued. "You must have heard their cant?"

"Indeed," I replied. I could not reconcile his educated manner with his grotesque appearance, although I imagine that Inspector Lea might have said the same about me.

"Now, shall we attend to our business?", the Gargoyle continued. "As Jegane observed, either you shall kill me, or I, you; I do hope that you find my choice of arena to your liking."

"It suits me well." I had caught my breath and my gauntleted fingers were scant inches away from the flash-trigger.

"Firstly, though, I'm sure that you have wondered 'why' and so-forth, and I shall elucidate," the monster said. "I know certain matters concerning you, Sir; not your real name, for he would not give that up, but between the Jemmies and myself, you have been under observation since you arrived in London. I know that in one of your guises you have befriended the wounded policeman Lea and his pretty sister. I have made your business my own and I have made use of it." He swung lightly on the ropes, raising up on the tips of his toes, flexing himself like a cat.

This was no time to consider the implications of this lunatic knowing my secrets and to question him would have put me at a disadvantage, but to whom had he referred – who "would not give that up"? No-one knew my real name, other than Ned Burrage and the masquers of the Hellfire Club.

"The truth is that I owe you thanks for inspiring me to take my craft to ever more theatrical heights. I am grateful, Jack. Now, however, a wealthy man wants you bumped off and I rather covet the seven-league boots upon your feet. Rest assured, I shall put them to the most artful use."

"This wealthy patron of yours – you speak of Roland Ashton."

"Quite so! I'm told that he prefers to keep his hands clean in these affairs, whereas myself … I crave dirty hands."

"Your confidence is a thing of wonder, Sir," I replied. "It will be my great pleasure to see you off, either to jail or to Hades."

"Perhaps, but first, I should like you to see something. It is a minor work, not really up to my usual standard, but I think that you shall appreciate it."

With that, the fiend released the rope from his right hand and behind him the sail dropped and flapped away into the darkness below, revealing the burnt and bleeding body of faithful Ned, his wrists cruelly bound together, hanging from a rope tied about his ankles.

"Your friend put up a decent fight, Jack, much better than all those little groundling girls, but he is old. He tired, and he was overcome, and then I trussed him, just like a Christmas goose, and had my pleasure of him. Still, he told me very little before, I shame to say, I lost my patience." With this, the Gargoyle reached into a pouch at his belt and drew forth a small, dark object that he cast towards my feet. It landed wetly and I saw that it was a human tongue.

At this, dark colours, reds and blacks twisted together like smoke, seemed to rise through my body and cloud my mind. I was almost lost to reason in my rage and crouched to spring at him, to knock this perversion from his perch and drown him in the Thames, when he spoke again:

"You will observe that Mr. Burrage is hanging from a rope, and that I hold the other end of that rope. When last I looked, he was still alive. Consider carefully, Jack."

He had me. The drop beneath Ned was close to seventy feet.

"You will now remove your boots and weapons, slowly but not too slowly, lest my arm should tire. And then I shall truss you up, Jack, truss you like a Christmas goose, and we shall look deep into you and see you for yourself."

Ned's body twisted in the wind, the rope creaking. I recalled my many debts to the old Sergeant and made the only choice I could.

With a mighty leap I sprang over the Gargoyle's head. Instantly he was aware of my movement, he released the rope, but I managed to catch it as it whipped upwards. Ned was heavier than I and his weight hauled me further into the sky, out of the Gargoyle's reach and up towards the broad, mast-like beam and the pulleys that supported us both. I turned upside-down like a bat, thankful for my long training upon the mallah-kambh, bracing both springs against the beam and halting my ascent.

Hooking my legs about the timber from beneath, I gripped hard to the rope and wound the slack about the pulley itself, jamming it tight. As Ned came to a juddering halt in space, I glanced down and saw the Gargoyle fling himself from the platform, aiming for the rope that held my friend. I dropped, somersaulting in mid-air; my boots hit the platform and I sprang after the madman, but I was an instant too late. He slashed out; the rope parted, and Ned plummeted down into the dark.

I tumbled with my enemy over the void and then we crashed down upon a bridge strung between this tower and the next. At the same moment came a splash from far below.

I scrambled to my feet and the Gargoyle did the same, his crushed face a mask of vicious glee.

"Well played, Jack! Now let us see if you are all your legend says!"

If Ned had survived the fall, he could not possibly survive long in the water. I moved to vault the railing and follow him down, but the Gargoyle blocked my way. He flourished his gloved hands at me like a wrestler, and now I perceived rows of wickedly curved talons projecting from steel bands across each of his palms. I had seen these weapons before; they were favoured by Indian assassins who sought to mask their murders as the attacks of wild beasts. These were the dreaded bagk-nakh, "tiger's claws."

Without pausing for thought, I flicked the flash-trigger and, as the Gargoyle flinched back against the incandescent burst, kicked him full in the chest with my right stilt. The spring-heel gave slightly on impact and his padded vest saved him from any real harm, but I drove from the hip and the blow was enough to send him reeling back along the narrow bridge, clutching at the railing. The claws of his right hand caught momentarily in my boot and I was dragged off-balance, falling against him.

We grappled, the Gargoyle still blinded by the magnesium flare. He slashed and gouged at me with his claws but could do no harm through the hardened leather panels of my armour; yet it was all that I could do to keep his talons away from my face and throat.

At such close-quarters, sight is not as important as other factors – weight, for one, in which I was at a distinct disadvantage, but also what Guru Alli spoke of as "feel", the knack of predicting an opponent's actions by subtle cues of pressure.

Threading my left arm between both of the Gargoyle's, I shifted my stance and shoved my forearm up against his left elbow, turning him off-balance and freeing my right hand to drive two short, steel-shod punches into his ribs. My enemy grunted and pulled partly away. I reached back to twist the valve that would release my ether jet, but before I could complete the movement he swung his arm down again, his forearm catching me a chopping blow to the side of my neck. He was monstrously strong and this blow sent me crashing through the railing, which splintered like kindling wood. I dropped through space and landed heavily on my side on the platform beneath.

Winded by the fall and half-stunned by the blow, I lay there for several seconds, trying to clear my vision. The Gargoyle, having recovered from the flare, plunged after me, landing astride my body. As he reared his claws back for the coup de grace, I managed to activate the valve switch and twin jets of blue mist enveloped his face. My enemy gagged and weakened and I rolled him off, hammering at him with both gauntlets and knocking off his hat, which flipped and spun down into the darkness. He shielded himself with the leather pads about his elbows like a boxer, gasped in fresh air and reeled back to his feet - evidently, his powers of recuperation were as extraordinary as his strength.

I leaped over the rail and off to an adjacent platform, but instead of pursuing me he vaulted over the railing on the opposite side, catching hold of a mooring rope and sliding down, vanishing almost soundlessly into the shadows below. I quickly glanced over the edge and, by the reflection of pale moonlight upon the brackish water, judged that we were still some sixty feet up. I could see nothing of poor Ned.

Then a light flared and I leaped down towards it, landing on one of the walkways that ran beneath the maze of platform towers. The Gargoyle stood a few yards away, brandishing a burning taper. He advanced upon me, and then suddenly drew the taper towards his face, exhaling a stream of some flammable liquid into a fiery fountain that sprang across the distance between us.

With no time to jump away, I turned and swung my capelet up to shield my face and eyes against the blast. In an instant, he was upon me again, snarling like a wild boar, his claws raking down the side of my mask and drawing blood from my cheek while he stabbed at me with the end of the burning taper.

As I reeled away he followed, raining down slashing gouges with his steel claws which drew sparks as they rebounded from my gauntlets, and swinging his torch which left dazzling, fiery trails through the gloom. In parrying a swing I tripped, one of my springs catching in a gap in the rough boards of the walkway, and he dove in, gripping my legs and dumping me bodily over the railing. Twisting violently in mid-air I seized his head in a chancery hold and hauled him over the edge with me.

We fell, locked together, for a few feet until I felt him hit something hard, perhaps one of the support beams; we rolled off and landed again some few feet lower, with the Gargoyle bearing the brunt of the fall. I heard him grunt as our impact forced the air from his lungs. Somehow he had retained his grip on the torch and now he dashed it up into my chin. I reared back, burned and cursing, and saw that we now stood on a makeshift platform of a few planks strung between a square formation of beams, part of the framework supporting the highest tower.

I jumped over his head and off onto the next level down, and he spun and leaped after me; so we continued, bounding and tumbling from one platform to the next as if down a gigantic staircase, striking blows as best we could, sometimes in mid-air, our momentum building to a lethal, breakneck speed.

I reached the final stage a full leap ahead of the Gargoyle and spread my cape, catching just enough wind to slow down, and bent my knees deeply, absorbing the shock of landing. I spun about just in time to meet him head-on. He flew towards me at a tremendous velocity, howling like a banshee, his claws ready to tear me apart; at the last instant I whirled aside and the madman hurtled past me, blasting through the guard rail and down into the bog beneath with an almighty splash.

I stepped to the edge, half expecting yet another assault; but when I peered down, breathless, burned and bruised, I saw him struggling in the black mud and sinking fast. He heaved and cast about for something with which to extricate himself, but there was nothing within reach, and in moments the frigid, stinking loam had sucked him under until nothing but his face remained above. At that moment he looked up at me, quite calmly.

"Do give my regards to the Inspector and his sister, Jack."

"Just keep sinking, would you?"

"I'll see you in Hell, " said the Gargoyle.

"Not if I should see you first," I replied, and then the mire took him.

I stayed a moment, until the roils and ripples had stilled. Then, with the rush of combat over, I was suddenly exhausted, truly bone-weary. Blisters formed about the burn on my chin and the blood pouring from my lacerated cheek soaked into my vest; my neck had been badly wrenched, several teeth felt loose and my head pounded.

I turned my back upon the bog and tried to ascertain where Ned might have fallen, knowing that, by now, there was no question of saving his life.

I was in no state to master my emotions; a black and soul-deep dread at what I'd find beneath the scaffold towers mingled with panic at the thought that the madman might also have brought harm to Charles and Catherine, or that Roland might have realised my true identity after all. Fighting to control my breath, I tried to channel it all, to fuel the search; yet the dark waters beneath the towers held their secrets.

Just then, a piercing whistle drew my attention out into the Thames. An agile skiff emerged from the gloom, close enough that I could clearly see its occupants; two men wearing flat caps, their lower faces concealed by bandannas, and a slight woman wearing a feathered guising mask with a short, hooked bill.

"Mistress Kestrel," I surmised aloud.

"Spring Heeled Jack," the river pirate replied. "The boy Charlie is safe and I want you to know that I played no part in his peril. Jegane tricked me as she tricked you, and she begs your forgiveness as she begged mine."

I assured the masked woman that I held no ill-will against her, nor Jegane; and together, we found Ned.

I shall not describe the ruin that had been made of that fine old soldier, except to say that I was tempted, in the hours that followed, to dig the Gargoyle's corpse out of the mire and visit upon it such injuries as he had done my friend. I take neither pride nor shame in this.

Suffice to say that I believe that Sergeant Ned Burrage had known that I was with him, toward the end; but Ned had died alone beneath the Victoria Dock tower, in the cold early morning of March 12th, 1866, and may Spring Heeled Jack be damned for that.

"You're owed a bounty," the Kestrel said somberly.

"Dispose of this man's mortal remains with dignity and we're square," I replied. "His name was Edward Burrage and a truer companion you could not hope to find."

"If I'd known that the monster had him …" the masked woman began, "… but the threat to the boy's life was real, and though it's a heavy price, you've done a great boon in ridding London of its Gargoyle. You've my word that your friend will be buried with all due honour."

Then we heard the splashing of approaching oars, and the Kestrel quickly turned, scanning the eddying fog for shadows.

"We'd best away, now - the River Police will be patrolling soon," she said. "I bid thee fare well, Spring Heeled Jack."

I took a deep breath as the Kestrel's skiff slipped away, and stinging tears rolled down my face.

Mustering my last vestiges of energy, I then made my way to the Lea residence in Camden Town. It was imperative that Charles and Catherine be warned that the Gargoyle had threatened them both. My qualms about appearing before them as Spring Heeled Jack were many and well-founded, but better that than their friend Jack Haining, his face a sorry mess of blood, burns and bruises, turning up at their doorstep in the pre-dawn hours with intelligence concerning the Gargoyle. As it turned out, this was a moot point because they were not at home, so I scribbled a letter to the Inspector and posted it their mailbox.

Inspector Lea,

I trust that this message finds you recovered from your wound.

The man who was responsible for the attack upon you and for the recent spate of killings and cruel assaults shall plague London no more. He is drowned in the mud of the Thames. This man was known to some as "the Gargoyle". If his death was not by my hand, then I may be forgiven a certain cold pride in reporting that I did nothing to prevent it, though it came at a great cost to me.

Should this be taken to comprise a written confession of murder on my part, then so be it. Frankly, I am past caring.

Please also be aware that the madman professed a threat against yourself and against your sister. Though he is dead and gone, others may yet present a danger towards you both. I deeply regret that this may be in some measure the result of your association with me and I entreat you to take extra care.

My business in London is not yet completed, nor shall I presume to hope that we need never meet again in a 'professional' capacity. Know that I hold you in the very highest esteem, Sir, and also that I regret that my mission henceforth shall brook no interference.

With my sincere regards,

I remain,

"Spring Heeled Jack"

At the bottom of this letter I sketched a map of where the Gargoyle's body could be found, in hopes that its recovery might offer some relief to the families of the girls who had been injured and slain by the madman. Lea had no particular cause to trust me in any of this, except that he knew that the man he had met upon the roof of the Opera House in Soho was not the lunatic who had nearly killed him, moments after.

That duty done I retired to an alley and doffed my mask and the most obvious of Spring Heeled Jack's accoutrements, bundling them in my cape, and hailed a cab to take me back to the vicinity of Wardour Street, for I dared not return to any of my hotels.

We arrived as the dawn was breaking. I paid the man and, as he pulled away, staggered into the graveyard. It took the last of my strength to climb atop the Crypt and my last memory of that awful night is that I pulled the hatch fast behind me.

Chapter 32

"Rooftop Murderer Found Dead in the Thames"
Suicide or Execution?

Inspector Aylward of the Metropolitan Police has this morning informed the Times that his constables have recovered the body of the man believed to have committed a string of outrageous assaults and foul murders over the recent weeks. The corpse was found buried in the mud at the site of a new extension to the Victoria Dock, and Inspector Aylward reports that the man appeared to have drowned.

The Inspector refused to comment when questioned about the precise circumstances of the man's death, leading to speculation that he was a suicide or that the murderer himself fell victim to some form of vigilante justice. However, the Inspector did confirm the presence of certain items recovered with the man's body, strongly indicating that he was, in fact, the villain believed to have been responsible for the murders of Miss Alice Masterson, whose body was discovered hanging from the London Exchange clock tower this Saturday last, and of Miss Polly Brown, similarly discovered in Soho two weeks past.

The body was identified by witnesses, including Miss Margaret Scales of Limehouse and Miss Emmeline Alsop of Bow, both of whom confirmed that they believed the man pulled from the mud to have been the same as he who had assaulted their sisters.

Police inquiries shall continue into the identity of the dead man, with one source commenting that he is believed to have been well-known amongst the criminal fraternity as a youth, and that he was transported for theft in the late '30s.

Inspector Aylward has declared the inquiry into the murders closed and also commented –

"I trust that these tragedies will put an end to the games of hoaxers who have delighted in frightening honest people by playing the Spring Heeled Jack."

Chapter 33

As exhausted as I was, I managed only a few hours of sleep, and those passed strangely. Upon awakening around mid-day, I immediately resolved to abandon the various civilian identities that I had assumed around London. If the Gargoyle, or even the Jemmies under duress, had passed any of his intelligence on to others in the criminal fraternity, then I was no longer safe in any of my aliases, for in my sporadic vigilantism I had made enemies of sundry thugs and bruisers, not to mention my duplicitous cousin and his bravos.

Worse still was the possibility that villains might take indirect vengeance against Spring Heeled Jack by harming Charles or Catherine, as the Gargoyle had harmed Ned. I looked forward to hearing from the Leas, hopefully sooner than later.

Better all around that Jack Haining should simply disappear – called away to tend for a sick relative in a distant part of the country, perhaps – and that Spring Heeled Jack be left to finish his business with Roland for good and all.

That afternoon I checked out of each of my hotels, excusing my facial injuries as the consequence of an assault by a tavern brawler. Once darkness fell I moved my few belongings into the Crypt, which would henceforth serve as Jack's sole base of operations.

My first order of business that night was to make the appropriate arrangements on behalf of poor Ned. He had no family that I knew of other than his elderly cousin Albert in Guildford, and I sent the fellow a note under yet another assumed name, informing him of Ned's passing without implicating him in the "crimes" of Spring Heeled Jack. As far as the old apothecary need know, Ned had died peacefully in his sleep, leaving a bequest – in fact, Ned's share of the Ashton Hall rent-money – to be distributed between his cousin and any other remaining family members.

I wrote another letter to a solicitor, engaging him to arrange for Ned's horses and carriage to be taken to the Guildford stables and cared for, there to await the return of his business partner, to whom they would be donated. From what Ned had told me, Edwin Hunt was a good man with a large family to care for; I trusted that the gift would ease his way.

With this, I felt that I had done all that I could for my friend.

I then wrote three further notes by the light of my small gas-lamp, one each to Charles and Catherine, and one to Frederick Barnes at the Alfredian Club, making my excuses as Jack Haining and wishing them all my very best. Absurdly, in that my relationships with all three had been based upon deception from the start, I felt badly about lying to them. They were good and admirable people and I would sorely miss their company, Catherine's most especially; yet I did not truly doubt that they would be better off without me.

These sad duties discharged, I found myself at a loose end. Other than a pounding headache, I seemed to have suffered no lasting harm in my encounter with the Gargoyle, and was recovering my strength and vim, but I fought to quell any desire to return to the rooftops that night. I shall admit that the decent part of me feared what I might do to any street miscreant that I happened across, for though the murderer was dead and gone, twists of red and black yet flickered through my mind, unbidden.

The natural outrage against against brutality undeservedly inflicted was somehow transformed within me into a desire to inflict brutality upon those who deserved it indeed, and London offered up no end of those.

That night my sleep was twice interrupted by vicious nightmares in which my enemy hauled himself from the Thames mud and demanded bloody vengeance. I awoke from these dreams with a start, sweating and tensed as if to fight, the cuts upon my cheek and the burn-wound on my chin throbbing as if freshly inflicted. I wondered whether the villain's claws had been coated with some form of poison, yet acting upon my mind.

I'd had enough of vigilantism in any case; hereafter my only mission was that of retribution, and Roland was my target.

Chapter 34

Ashton House, facing Soho Square, was an imposing edifice of five stories. The ground level was leased to retailers, at present a tobacconist and a milliner; the two levels above housed offices for the administration of the Ashton estate, the next was servants' quarters, and the top two levels were reserved for family use. I well recalled the various rooms from my visits there as a child, though as I had grown older, my father had been content to leave the nuts and bolts of his business interests to his staff, and we had visited London less frequently.

My extensive prior surveillance of the House had confirmed that Roland was occupying the master suite on the top floor, and that at least one of his bodyguards was sequestered in the servants' rooms, two floors beneath. All told, I could expect active resistance from several quarters should I mount a direct assault upon the House, and that is not to mention the Peelers who would surely be alerted at the first sign of trouble.

None of this was of any great concern to me; going by his behaviour to date, there seemed no chance that Roland would give himself away unless offered no alternative. I would have to take the great risk that his forced confession, supported by the revelation of my true identity to the appropriate authorities, would be enough to secure my safety and the return of what was rightfully mine.

On the night of March 15th, at the hour of ten o'clock, I followed Roland home from the Inns of Court and ascertained that only one of his bull-necked bodyguards accompanied him from his carriage and into Ashton House. The area about Soho Square was well-illuminated by gas-lamps, and I had long observed that the light from these lamps blurred the vision of those at street-level to any events taking place high above them.

I sprang out over the street, bounced once and thence up on top of the adjacent building, which happened to be a small theatre, then set myself to climbing the remaining three levels to the roof of Ashton House. After a few strenuous minutes I was perched atop the House and awaiting my moment to strike.

Peering through the great sky-light, I noted that the master suite was still dark and so settled in to wait. Perhaps five more minutes passed before the chamber was lit by a gaslight glow. Roland was there, beneath me and alone; the time had come. I sprang high into the air and came down feet-first against the sky-light, smashing it to smithereens and plummeting into the master-suite in a shower of shattered glass.

Roland was in his dressing gown when I made my entrance and his first reaction was to bolt for the door leading to the stairwell. I sprang over his head and arrived there before him, shoving him back into the room. He staggered, but did not fall, and I hauled a bookshelf down to bar the door. Then I spun about to face him, expecting him to cry out for help – but we could both already hear the commotion from below stairs. I would have to be quick.

"Spring Heeled Jack, yes? And what is the meaning of this outrage?"

"No outrage here, 'Sir' Roland. The outrage was committed months ago, against your cousin."

At this Roland flinched, but composed himself instantly.

"I've no idea what you mean. If it's more of my money you're after, then …"

"You bore false witness against Jack Ashton and allowed him to be put to death. You have been living a lie, 'Sir' Roland, and your hired assassin is drowned in mud; now it is time to pay the Devil his due." He backed away as I advanced upon him, milling his fists in tense imitation of a pugilistic guard and glancing again towards the door. From below, there came muffled shouts and the sounds of heavy footsteps upon the wooden stairs.

"Why do you care? What is my cousin's fate to you?" He was buying time. Hammering, now, at the door.

"You will confess your perjury. You will abandon your claim to the Ashton estate. You, Sir, will speak the truth of this matter, or you will die by the hand of Spring Heeled Jack!" With this snarled threat I leapt at him, knocking him to the floor and seizing his throat in both steel-shod hands.

"All right! All right, I admit it! But it was not I who engineered the plot!"

"Who, then? Who else stood to gain by your treachery?"

The door began to splinter under the force of heavy blows. I drew my gauntleted fist back for the coup de grace. Roland's eyes widened in fear, then squeezed tightly shut.

"Speak the name or I will send you to Hell!"

"Manfred, damn you!" he cried. "It was Colonel Eustace Manfred!"

At this the door finally burst open. I swung about, poised to fight, and beheld a giant of a man shoving the fallen bookshelf out of his path; he raised a pistol and I sprang away just as he fired. His aim was wide, and I reached for the flash-trigger upon my belt, when suddenly I realised that he had shot Roland!

I looked back to where my cousin lay, and saw for the first time that he, too, was clutching a pistol – the bodyguard had likely saved my life.

"Ashton! Jack Ashton!" the bodyguard shouted. "I will do ye no harm!" He kept his weapon leveled at Roland, but the erstwhile Lord of Ashton Hall was faltering and dropped his hand, the pistol falling from his grip.

"You bloody fool … shoot the devil …" he gasped.

"Nay, m'Lord, for he is worth ten of you." The bodyguard stepped into the room, kicking aside the books that lay scattered at his feet.

At this, Roland's eyes focussed again upon me.

"Jack?" he said. "Jack … Ashton?" He was panting now, his face creasing into a mask of dread and bitter anger.

"It cannot be. Jack died on the scaffold, I saw him hanged ... who are you? Who ... are you ..."

Seemingly of their own volition, my hands went to the buckle beneath my chin, and I removed the scarlet mask of Spring Heeled Jack. Roland's eyes grew wide again, then glazed. He was dead.

"That's twice I've saved your life, lad." The burly guard had come up behind me. I turned towards him, nonplussed, and he fetched me a backhanded blow to the jaw that sent me reeling and crashing into the wall.

"And that's one I owe you for biting me 'and. You've led us a merry chase, Mr. Spring 'eeled Jack."

I could scarce take all of this in, but finally recognised my brutish saviour – it was Vinegar Tom, likewise unmasked! He had a ruddy complexion, reddish mutton chop sideburns and, presently, a consternated cast to his broad features. The big man pocketed his weapon and started to speak again, when we heard another commotion from downstairs – shouting, and the harsh ratcheting noise of a Peeler's rattle.

"Right, you'd best be off. I'll 'andle this mess. I'll be in a carriage outside the Mug and Bow in Charing Cross Lane, tomorrow night, 8 o'clock. We're long overdue for a chat."

More men were pounding up the stairs, but I confess that I stood stunned by this unexpected turn of events.

"Go, damn you! I'll explain everything, but get out! There is no time! They must not see you here!"

I leapt up through the sky-light and away into the darkness, more amazed, I think, than ever before in my life.

Chapter 35

The next night found me waiting atop the Mug and Bow until a likely-looking grey coach pulled up outside. The man I knew only as Brother Vinegar Tom stepped out and scanned the street; I did the same and then, satisfied as to the absence of either witnesses or a Hellfire Club brute squad, I vaulted over the ledge, landing some distance off and in the middle of the lane. I did not care to startle the big man, who was sure to be armed and quick on the draw. But Tom simply motioned me into the cab, called for the driver to pull out and then immediately began to talk.

"All right, ask me your questions and be quick about it. We've a great deal to talk through."

I removed my mask and began to speak.

"As you say. Firstly, how did you come to be posing as Roland's bodyguard?"

"Trying to find you, me boy. We'd put two and two together – your grudge against Roland Ashton, then you abscond and next thing a bloody leaping demon is harassing Roland's men. I hired on with 'is crew in 'opes you'd do as you just did."

"I had no further options," I said wearily.

"Aye, so I understand. Now, mark me well - last week, we got word from a street informant that the rooftop maniac – what did they call him, the Gargoyle? – was offering to sell Master Spring'eel's secrets to the 'ighest bidder. Roland bid and won, of course, and then paid 'andsomely again to have the madman put an end to you. He was livid when 'e 'eard that was money wasted."

"My money, in point of fact," I replied. "The Gargoyle's death was an accidental suicide, in the act of trying to do me in. I watched him go."

"Good riddance to 'im," Tom offered. "Roland bought bits and pieces of intelligence, but not, of course, that Spring Heeled Jack was his cousin back from the grave. That leaves us with an ace in the hole."

"But the Gargoyle did know of my friendship with Charles Lea, the police Inspector, and his sister Catherine …"

Tom suddenly sat forward as the carriage rounded a sharp turn. A smaller man would probably have lost his balance.

"Aye, and that has put them in dire straits," he said urgently.

"I visited their home that very night to warn them, but they were out," I told him. "I left a note explaining the peril and warning they take extra care."

"You've not seen a newspaper since that night?" Tom asked.

"No – what are you getting at?"

"The Hellfire Club 'as agents within the Metropolitan police, instructed to report any news of yourself or of the Gargoyle. Part of our efforts to track you down. Two days ago we got word that Lea hadn't reported for duty. The constables found yer note in their mailbox but there was no sign of Lea himself, nor of 'is sister. They've disappeared altogether."

I cursed myself as a selfish fool for not making damned certain that the Leas were safe. If they'd come to some harm on my account, I should never forgive myself.

"My God – if the Gargoyle sold my secrets four or five days ago …"

"Aye, it's grim. Manfred himself has taken them."

"So Roland was telling the truth?"

Tom scowled. "Your Colonel Manfred is a dangerous man right now; a very dangerous man. Yes, it was the Colonel's idea to have you stitched up for treason and it was he who 'ad those papers forged and all. The deal was that Roland could have what 'e liked of your father's fortune here in England, but 'e was to give Manfred control of the estate in India. And that, young Ashford, is just what 'appened."

"The Colonel was like a second father to me."

"He's venom and fangs, lad."

"You must know that he's visiting London …" I began, but Tom cut me off.

"Of bleedin' course we do! Manfred doesn't know that Jack Ashton is alive and well, thank God, but he might 'ave agreed with Roland that the Spring Heeled Jack was getting too close." Tom glanced out the window, seemingly lost in thought for a moment.

"And then," I ventured, "had Charles and Catherine abducted as security against the chance of his plot being discovered."

"Just so, and there's worse still. You brace yourself for this, you understand? I need you to keep a clear head."

"Tell me."

Tom drew a deep breath.

"Your father's death was no act of nature, Jack. Manfred's men made it appear so."

I could not speak. Tom looked penetratingly into my eyes, then nodded and continued, speaking at a rapid clip.

"The Hellfire Club is independent, but right now, we're working as agents of the Crown. We were keeping a quiet eye on the situation in India – unofficial, like – which is 'ow we caught wind of Manfred's scheme. Too late, I'm sorry to say, for us to save your father."

Even as we spoke, I could not fathom Manfred's cunning and duplicity; how long had he been leading this double-life as honourable officer and base villain?

"He's very clever, is the Colonel, but then so are we," Tom continued. "Anyroad, we reckoned the best way to put a stop to 'im was to give 'im enough rope, as t'were. If he thought you dead, he'd set his plans in motion, and then we could reveal him for the blackguard he was, 'ave 'im put away nice and legal. You turnin' up alive was to be our ace, Sir."

"And how the hell would you have explained my resurrection to the rest of the world?"

"The plan was to keep you safe and quiet 'til Manfred tipped his hand, reveal your real identity to the proper authorities at the right time, then set you up under a false name somewhere out of the way – you'd 'ave kept your fortune, just not as Sir John Ashton."

"I'd have had something to say about that!"

"Aye, no doubt you would, and all," Tom growled. "Things 'ave, to put it mildly, Sir, 'changed' since you decided to go leaping about on your own. Months, we've lost now! Manfred's plans have proceeded without a hitch. We missed our moment and now it's all arse-backwards. Meself, I wish we'd just bumped the bastard off back when we could 'ave gotten close enough, but at the time that was deemed bad form."

"I still don't see why the Hellfire Club got involved, let alone the Crown. So Colonel Manfred would have gained my lands in India – how is that of such vital import to the British Government?"

"Do you have any inkling of just how wealthy your father was, lad? It's not just land, though that's enough; it's stocks, businesses, a vast fortune. With that backing, Manfred plots to revive the cult of the Thuggee, the Phansigars; then he'll set them against the Crown."

The carriage careened around a corner with a thundering rattle of hooves on cobblestones.

"The Strangler cult?" I exclaimed. "You can't be serious. Sleeman and his lot put paid to them years ago!"

"Aye, so they'd like you to believe. Major-general Sleeman did them damage, stripped their coffers almost bare, but it wasn't enough. The truth of it is that their leaders, the top men, survived the purge. They've changed tactics now; no more roving packs of bandits waylaying travellers in the wilds, no, Sir. They've gotten bloody political. They 'ave agents all over now, assassin networks built up over the past thirty years – China, Burma, even some cells over 'ere. Many in 'igh places, or close to those who are. They could seize control of damned near every native regiment."

"Good God, another rebellion?!"

"India's a tinderbox, lad! With Manfred's backing, our troops wouldn't stand much of a chance against them. Even aside from the military threat, their Thugs could wipe out most of the British Governors, half our Generals and a good half-dozen of the House of Lords before breakfast.

If they win, he'll be in league with the new rulers of India. If they start to lose, he'll turn on them and come out of it as the hero who quelled the uprising. Either way, the Empire cannot cede control of the Raj to a man like Colonel Manfred."

He glanced out the window again, and, following his gaze, I saw that we were turning into Leadenhall Street. The carriage was slowing.

"Just up ahead, Sir," the carriageman reported.

Tom paused then and sat back in his seat, presumably to let all of this sink in, for which I was sincerely grateful. Colonel Manfred, not only the would-be architect of my own death – twice, if Tom's intuition about the Gargoyle was correct - but the man behind my father's demise as well, and a traitor to the Crown on an unimagined scale. If he had harmed Charles or Catherine …

"All right, Tom. With Roland dead – and I thank you for that – I can see no course forward but to help the Hellfire Club in covert service to Her Majesty. My first duty, though, must be to see to my friends' safety. What can I do?"

"We're doin' it now, lad," said Tom soberly. "The Colonel is attending a conference in Whitechapel tomorrow, nutting out military escort protocols for traders in the Southern provinces. Our Clubmen 'ave arranged for certain other dignitaries – key men, you understand – to be present there. All you need to do is stay hidden until the time is right, then show them Jack Ashton's face.

Tonight, though, Manfred's stayin' in his private apartment, yonder at East India House. Lea and 'is sister are held within."

I recognised the imposing bulk of the East India building, some way down the road.

"Find 'em, then get 'em out 'ere smartish and as quiet as you can, savvy?" Tom insisted, as the carriageman turned his horses down a shadowy alley. "And 'ave a care - Manfred's known to 'ave 'is best men with 'im. Fanatics, the lot of them."

The carriage proceeded some yards further through the gloom, until Tom rapped on the roof, bringing us to a halt. I took a deep breath, then again donned my devilish mask.

As I stepped out, Tom dropped his heavy hand upon my shoulder. I turned back and he allowed himself a wry grin. "Bloody Spring Heeled Jack, eh? I'll 'and it to yer, young Master Ashton, you 'ave some brass."

Chapter 36

Three swift leaps carried me to the end of the alley and half-way up the wall of a shuttered fire station. I climbed the remaining distance to the roof, then bounded back across the gabled expanse to a convenient perch overlooking Leadenhall Street and East India House. Within would be a warren of unknown rooms and hallways; Charles and Catherine might be anywhere. My obvious tactic was to coerce intelligence of their whereabouts from a likely lackey.

I instantly judged the roof of that august establishment at least one floor too high to reach with a spring, and I knew from long experience that this type of stone edifice could neither easily nor quickly be scaled. So it was that, by traversing from one building to the next and assessing various points of ingress, I arrived finally atop a high brick wall at the rear of the House, which – typical of that area, in those days – enclosed a stable-yard. The barn across the yard butted about half way up against the rear wall of the main building; here, then, was my way in.

The yard was well lit by lanterns and quite lively with activity. Crouching in the shadows, I timed my next leap carefully between the coming and goings of the stable-boys and then sprang forth, bouncing twice diagonally across the yard and landing atop the hay-barn, albeit narrowly saving myself from falling through an open hatch. Glancing through it, I took a moment to appreciate the horses stabled below – magnificent beasts, most of them, and the least was still many cuts above the average London workhorse.

Now out of sight from those at ground level, and hearing no alarums, as Shakespeare would have it, I stepped across the roof and approached the nearest window with some stealth. It would not do to be spotted. The room within was dark; I allowed myself a quick glance through the pane, gleaning the impression that it was unoccupied. Short of scraping away the putty, though, there was no quiet way in, so instead I climbed up past the window, crawling, bat-like, forking the tines of my gauntlets and steel-shod feet into the crevices between the stones. This was laborious and unsure work, but it eventually gained me access to a second-story window ledge – likewise, dark and with no signs of observers within - and then a third. All were locked, of course, so I proceeded up to the roof, thinking to borrow a trick from the hated Gargoyle and enter via the chimney flue, if all else failed.

As I raised my face over the ledge, though, I was happy to see the moonlit expanse of roofscape interrupted by a large hatchway; typical of buildings of this vintage, it was undoubtedly used by caretakers. Locked from within, of course, but the boards were easily prised away and soon I was able to drop down into a dark, narrow, low-ceilinged service corridor.

I folded my springs back to allow easier and quieter movement in this close space, then padded along on India-rubber soles, largely feeling my way, my ears keenly alert to any sound. In short order I discovered a second hatchway, which lifted to reveal a ladder down; the room below was illuminated only by moonlight streaming in through the window.

Clambering down, I heard muffled footsteps; the next room, or the next after that, was clearly occupied. Then the sound of a door opening, and footsteps on a wooden floor, moving away from me. I eased out in silent pursuit and found myself in a hall whose windows overlooked the lantern-lit stableyard, now three stories below. Ahead of me walked a slight man, whose years I could not tell from behind, but from his dress I judged him to be a servant.

No time for diplomacy. I matched his footsteps with longer strides and caught up with him just as he was turning a corner, clamping my chainmailed palm over his mouth to stifle his shocked cry and hauling him back down the corridor and into the ladder room. There I turned him about and thrust him hard against the wall; his eyes bugged as he beheld the devil-mask of Spring Heeled Jack.

"Speak soft, if you value sleeping in a whole skin," I hissed at him. "I seek a man and a woman, Charles and Catherine Lea, who are prisoners in this House. Tell me – where might they be?"

The servant sputtered, but he did speak softly. "I ... I could not say ... I mean, I don't know, S-sir. Prisoners at East India House? I'm sorry, I'm sorry, please do not hurt me ..."

I believed him by the look in his eyes, thought quickly, and then demanded: "Guests, then? Guests of Colonel Manfred, or members of his party? Guests whom the servants have not seen?"

"Y-yes, the Colonel's two friends who are unwell, a tropical ailment ... please, Sir, I b-beg you to leave them be, for they are very ill ...".

"Where?"

"S-sir, they are quartered on the s-second floor, n-next to the Colonel's apartment ..."

"They shall come to no harm by my hand," I told the man, and then I put him to sleep with a jet of ether. The fellow seemed blameless; he would awaken, groggy but unharmed, in perhaps half an hour's time and I trusted that I would be well away by then.

Proceeding quietly back down the corridor and turning the corner I beheld another hallway, and so made my way until I came, inevitably, to a broad staircase leading down. Charles and Catherine would surely be under close guard, possibly drugged, and I was mindful of Tom's warning that the Colonel's best men were with him; this would be no easy rescue.

I crept down the stairs and carefully peered around the corner, whereupon I beheld two tall, heavily bearded Indians standing to attention at either side of a central doorway; both of them were bristling with weapons. I slowly drew myself back into concealment, well aware that gradual movement is far less apt to attract the notice of a wary eye.

The brilliant blue of their high turbans and loose bana shirts, criss-crossed with orange sashes, had confirmed my darkest intuitions – Manfred's mercenary guards were Nihang, the elite fighting men of the Sikh. All Nihang were trained in the myriad arts of war, virtually from birth; to this day, I know of no deadlier opponents in hand-to-hand combat. I reckoned that I should be able to defeat one, even in such confined quarters as the corridor, but against two, even if I could avoid being slashed to ribbons, the affray would surely rouse all of East India House against me.

The trick here, I realised, would be to persuade my enemies to bring their captives to me. I offered a silent apology to Vinegar Tom, for this would be no stealthy rescue.

Chapter 37

Moments later, perched atop the roof, I readied my smoke grenades for instant action and then leapt over the edge, plunging a dangerous distance down into the street below. As the rebound shot me up again I pegged a grenade through a second story window, then another and another as I continued to bound along; now three more grenades hurled through windows of the ground floor. Immediately following the crash of shattering glass, cries were raised, and even more so as clouds of scarlet smoke began billowing from the broken windows.

One more leap carried me to a second-story balcony, where I turned around and called across the street, in the direction of the fire station; "Fire! Fire at East India House!" I then set about the arduous task of climbing the wall to the roof, gambling that this would attract no undue attention in the midst of the general uproar and under the cover of smoke and foggy darkness.

Upon reaching the rooftop, I glanced back towards the fire station and saw, to my considerable relief and satisfaction, the great doors opening and signs of excited activity from within. At that instant, however, I heard a high-pitched whine and was then dealt a blow to the back of my padded leather helmet that nearly pitched me over the edge again.

Spinning about, I saw a Nihang moving towards me across the roof from the direction of the hatchway, running silently in the low, crouch-legged gait that characterised his breed of fighting man. Of greater concern was the chakram that he was presently twirling around his upraised index finger as he zig-zagged towards me. I barely had time to settle into a fighting stance before he loosed the weapon, which whined through the air towards me; a flat steel quoit the width of a small dinner plate, edges honed sharp enough to sever a man's hand from his wrist. I had reason again to be thankful for the tough leather panels within my helmet and for my steel gauntlets, which I now used to bat away the Nihang's second missile; it ricocheted off into the darkness.

No more than fifteen feet away from me now, he unfurled from about his waist an urumi whip-sword, whirled it once about his head and then lashed it at me at full charge, the four long, flexible steel blades snaking out like the tentacles of the fabled hydra. I leapt straight over the attack and pirouetted in mid-air, thrusting my right spring-stilt hard into the man's back as I dropped and sending him flying headfirst over the edge of the roof, to land with a clattering crash on the balcony below.

I spared the man a glance and judged him unconscious if he were lucky. Then came more cries and commotion from within, and as I looked down the front doors of the East India building burst open, spilling an agitated crowd of servants and other staff out into Leadenhall Street. Across the way, fire brigadiers were wheeling two of their great pump engines out of the barracks, and some of the servants ran to help them.

Stealthily, meanwhile, Vinegar Tom's grey carriage was easing out from the broad alleyway adjacent to the fire station. I could only hope that Tom intuited the gist of my plan.

Within a few minutes, the brigadiers' hoses were blasting great jets of water in through the shattered windows, while a team armed with axes entered the front doors and, presumably, began searching for stragglers. I reckoned that I had five minutes at most before my ruse was revealed.

Having ascertained that no Nihang, nor boxes nor bundles large enough to contain human beings were to be seen down in the street, I bounded across the rooftop and surveyed the stable yard at the rear of the building. Sure enough, there were Charles and Catherine Lea, gagged and bound in the Indian fashion, being forced into a carriage by several Nihang guards. Two others prepared their horses to ride, and, as I watched, Colonel Manfred himself strode into view below me, followed by an attendant bearing an iron-tipped bamboo lance, the Colonel himself bellowing orders in rough Punjabi and strapping a brass cuirass about his barrel chest.

Seeing my friends so treated, my first impulse was to spring down and fight, but as manly as that action might have been, against those odds it would surely also have meant my doom and the Leas' continued capture. No, I should not commit myself now to folly. Biding my time, I watched and counted the Nihang; one driving the carriage, one inside keeping watch on Charles and Catherine and two mounted escorts. The Colonel, also, swung up into a saddle, then hoisted his lance and called his order; "We ride for the London Docks!"

Manfred's stratagem was clear; to transport his prisoners to one of the East India Company's berthed ships, there to keep them secure until he had concluded his business with the Leaping Demon of Soho. Well, that chance would come sooner than he knew.

Chapter 38

With a clattering of heavy hooves and rumbling of wagon wheels against the cobblestones, the Colonel's team began the three-mile journey to the Docks, turning into Billiter Street, right into Fenchurch Avenue and then into Lime Street. Other traffic was light at this time of the evening.

I kept pace with them along the rooftops, calculating my first play. More pressing even than my urge for vengeance against the duplicitous Colonel Manfred was the need to protect Charles and Catherine from harm; therefore, I must disable the men on the carriage with them.

The Colonel rode ahead of the carriage, and the two guards behind. I waited for Manfred to turn the corner into narrow Fenchurch Street and then cast two spark bombs down at the feet of the horsemen to the rear. Their steeds shied away from the flash and crackle of crimson gunpowder and I sprang down onto the roof of the carriage.

The driver began to turn and draw his tulwar sword, but I kicked him full in the face, sending him plummeting from his seat and crashing to the pavement.

"Look you there, it's the Spring Heeled Jack!" came a cry from a startled pedestrian.

Immediately the Nihang horsemen behind us shouted out, "Bole So Nihal, Sat Sri Akal!" - the famous Sikh battle-cry, promising victory to those who called the true name of God. Be that as it may, they could not encourage their horses through the smoke and sparks and the Colonel, having already turned the corner, could not offer them immediate assistance.

Wrenching open the ceiling hatch, I dropped inside and found the guard with his wickedly curved kirpan knife held menacingly to Catherine's throat. As he began to speak a dire threat, I slammed my chain-mailed palm into the elbow of his blade-wielding arm - striking the weapon away from Catherine and driving its point into the upholstery - then backhanded him across the face with the full weight of my armoured gauntlet and slung him headfirst through the door. Then, pulling the kirpan from its embedment, I sliced the ropes that held brother and sister Lea.

The carriage gave a sudden lurch as the skittish and masterless horses, having rounded the corner into Fenchurch Street, began to panic. I heard the shouts of onlookers from the pavements and suddenly, at both windows appeared the turbaned heads of the mounted Nihang warriors.

"We can drive!" Charles yelled as soon as his mouth was clear of the gag. "Go, man, keep us covered! We'll ride for the London Bridge!"

"Are you all right?" I asked Catherine. Before she could reply, a shining chakram whirred through the open window to my left, carving the air between us and chopping into the opposite door jamb.

"I'm fine, you bloody lunatic!" she shouted in reply. "Go, go!"

I scrambled up through the hatch and took quick stock of our situation. The driver and the carriage guard were out of the picture, but the two horsemen to either side of the now dangerously careening carriage were twirling their chakrams. The street behind them was filling up with erstwhile spectators, now trying to make heads or tails of the dangerous novelty London was offering this evening, some of them running to follow the carriage.

A short distance up ahead, Colonel Manfred was wheeling his mount about, clearly preparing to ride back. We could not possibly defend the carriage against an attack by a trio of armed horsemen, so we must keep moving!

As the Leas clambered up through the hatch and set about taking the reins, I sprang onto an adjacent shop awning. Instantly, a chakram flashed through the night air, chipping into the masonry barely a foot to my left. Bounding along the awning, I swatted away a second gleaming projectile, which struck golden sparks off my steel glove.

I leaped down into the street, bounced once and then sprang up onto the low rooftop of a haberdasher's shop, hoping to draw their fire - but then there came an anguished cry from Charles Lea, who slumped at the reins, a chakram embedded in his shoulder.

As Charles fell against his sister, he heaved on the reins and the horses ran sharply to the left, suddenly cutting off one of the pursuing Nihang. Seconds later, there came a terrific crash and clatter and the protesting screams of horses from the street below, followed by a great cry from the onlooking crowd on the footpaths.

The swerving carriage had forced the two pursuing riders into a collision. One man and horse lay in a tangle - as I watched, the horse climbed back to its feet, but the man lay still - while the other man was being dragged by his mount across the cobbles, one foot caught in the stirrup. Bystanders rushed to their aid. Meanwhile, Catherine took the reins and spurred the carriage horses into as full a gallop as could be managed, forcing Manfred to turn his steed about again and ride ahead of the onrushing coach.

Suddenly there was a loud bang and I felt the air part close by my face - he was firing back upon us! This brought startled cries of "Fetch the constables!" from men on both sides of the rapidly-clearing road.

The coach swung the corner into Gracechurch Street and I jumped down again, alighting upon the roof.

"Lea, are you badly hurt?"

"I'll live," he replied grimly, "provided we can fight our way out of this!" He was about to say more, but could only grit his teeth in pain. I judged the circular blade to have penetrated an inch into the back of his left shoulder, probably lodging in the bone - a bad and bloody wound, enough to make driving impossible, but his sister was keeping up the family name in that department.

"The next corner takes us onto King William Street," Catherine reported urgently. "I must slow down to make the turn. If Manfred can gain control of these horses ..."
"Drive as fast as you dare," I replied. "I'll keep him busy."

I leaped from the carriage and raced along the adjacent rooftops, barely, even with my mighty springs, able to keep ahead of the horses. Sure enough, just up ahead, where Gracechurch met Cannon Street, Manfred had turned his horse about to meet the carriage head-on, one pistol drawn and another holstered at the ready, with his iron-tipped bamboo lance and sabre sheathed in reserve. Pedestrians scattered away from the armoured soldier.

"Colonel!" I shouted, "we have business to attend!"

With a snarl, he took aim at me and fired, but I was already gone, leaping away, bouncing off the roof of a parked coach and then across the street, vaulting the rail of a fire escape. One of my spring stilts slipped between the grille bars and I was suddenly, momentarily trapped; he shot at me twice more, bullets ricocheting off the brick wall to either side, before turning his attention back to the onrushing carriage ... but he was an instant too late!

Catherine took the corner into Cannon Street at breakneck speed and, as the carriage sped past the Colonel, it tipped ominously onto two wheels. Horse and rider both started back; Manfred, recovering quickly, fired another shot, but it passed harmlessly through the carriage walls.

Wrenching my spring free, I vaulted the railing again, bounced twice across the street and just managed to catch the carriage door jamb. Catherine's speed was such that I was forced to run alongside, taking three great, bounding steps, before I could haul myself through the door; any man not equipped with my spring boots would have been torn free and rolled under the thundering wheels. With a vile, booming curse, Manfred spurred his horse into fast pursuit as Catherine drove hell-for-leather.

Gasping and drenched in sweat, I collapsed onto the seat. Although, by the luck of the Devil, I remained uninjured, my nerves were strained to their uttermost; and yet, the danger was far from over, for we were pursued by a monster onto London Bridge.

"Spring Heeled Jack!" Catherine called out, but then her words were drowned by a staccato volley of pistol shots - one, two-three, four-five. The fourth shot shattered the window over my head, showering me with shards of glass. The fifth left a neat hole high up in the opposite wall and, to my horror, I heard Catherine cry out in pain. Moments later, blood began to trickle through the bullet hole.

As I started to my feet and towards the ceiling hatch to help Catherine, the carriage began to careen wildly, smashing into one stone balustrade and then across to the other, flinging me about helplessly inside the cab. Plunging towards the left-side door, I glimpsed a hail of sparks sheared from the wheel hubs and I was overwhelmed by the vivid stench of burning iron. We swung back across the bridge and this time there was a terrific crunch, as the balustrade met wooden spokes; then the world roared and tumbled and went black.

Chapter 39

I opened my eyes, could not focus them, closed them, opened them again. The swimming shapes and colours resolved themselves into a dented oak panel and I realised that my head had made the dent; if not for my padded helmet, the blow would certainly have killed me.

I shifted, experimentally, and found that I was lying mostly on my right side, against the juncture where two walls met the ceiling of the upturned carriage. Both doors had been torn away and the opposite corner of the roof staved in by the crash, but I seemed unharmed other than a stiff neck and a pounding headache.

I crawled up and out the nearest doorway, past one of the horses which lay dead of a broken neck, its hindquarters pinned grotesquely beneath the flipped and wrecked cab. A pool of blood glistened darkly in the lamp-light. I stripped off my right gauntlet and touched the horse, confirming that it was still warm - I had been unconscious for only a moment. A backward glance through splintered wheel spokes and thickening fog revealed the glowering presence of Colonel Manfred, reining in his steed some dozen yards behind, calculating his next play.

The wooden shafts connecting carriage to team had snapped cleanly in half and of the other horse, there was no sight - nor, I realised with mounting dread as I clambered to my feet, seemed there to be any sight of Charles nor Catherine Lea. Ahead on the bridge, though, several carriages had halted and their drivers and passengers, some dozen in all, were running towards the wreck, to offer what help they could. I knew then that they could not yet see me, for surely they would not rush to the aid of the Leaping Demon of Soho …

Keeping a wary eye, for I was well within range of the Colonel's pistol shot, I stepped into the deepest shadow of the mangled carriage, hoping to confuse my enemy's aim and to forestall discovery by the approaching crowd. I called back:

"I am all right, but the man and the woman who drove this carriage - did you see what has become of them?"

"Over the edge and into the Thames", a man shouted. "I can just see 'em in the water - oh, Lord help them, I think they're drowning! Hang on! Hang on, you two! We'll fetch you a rope!"

"Both are injured!" I cried in reply, as Manfred spurred forward a step, then another.

"A rope, a rope!" went up the cry, and moments later I heard a splash.

"Can you get the loop around her, Sir?", another voice called, but then, "God's blood, it's no good - the current's got them!"

The would-be rescuers rushed as one to the downstream side of the bridge and cast their line again. I tensed myself to spring to my friends' aid, but instantly realised that would be suicidal; even if I had the fortune to dodge the Colonel's fire and leap into the water, my spring stilts would drag us all down to a silty grave. Wretched, wretched luck; was this the Devil come to take his due at last? Were Charles and Catherine to fall victim to my lunatic mission, at the very brink of its completion?

No! There was nothing for it; I must take the moment.

Colonel Manfred continued to advance his horse and my gaze fell upon the chakram, still embedded in the carriage door jamb. Wrenching it free, I sprang forth from the shadows, and immediately the Colonel raised his weapon; but I mimicked the Nihang's zig-zag run, leaping this way and that, and he could not draw proper aim in the gloom and fog. He fired twice into my advance, drawing cries from the rescuers:

"Who shoots?"

"See there - a soldier! Who's he up against?"

Then I flung the razor-edged quoit. Manfred ducked in the saddle and came up firing yet again - but he had spent his ammunition, and was rewarded only with a dry click.

More shouts, now, from the coachmen and their erstwhile passengers, crowded beneath a lamp-post:

"There, there - she's got it now! Hold fast, Miss!"

The Colonel's eyes blazed and I fancied that I could see his moustache bristle.

"Brave lad," he rumbled, spurring forward a step, "but it is all for naught. Once you're done, I shall take personal charge of that rescue. The policeman and his sister will not live to tell tales."

"Then fight your way past me, you dog, if that is within your power!" I snarled at him, "but you'd best make quick work of it!"

He sneered at my taunt, but in the next moment he heard what I had just seen, and quickly turned his head to behold a great mass of people and a grey carriage, led by a speeding Black Maria coach and flanked by mounted policemen, surging toward us from the City.

When he turned back toward me his eyes were lit with spiteful glee.

"I am a Colonel of the Queen's Lancers and you are nothing but a penny dreadful hobgoblin!" Manfred growled. "That eager mob will rip you limb from limb, and you've nowhere to run. All your bluff talk be damned!"

A distant clamor, now, as carriage wheels, horses' hooves and the shod feet of a hundred Londoners raced onto the bridge.

Manfred was right, curse him - but there was no choice other than to play this scene out to its bitterest end. While I lived, he would not reach Charles and Catherine Lea.

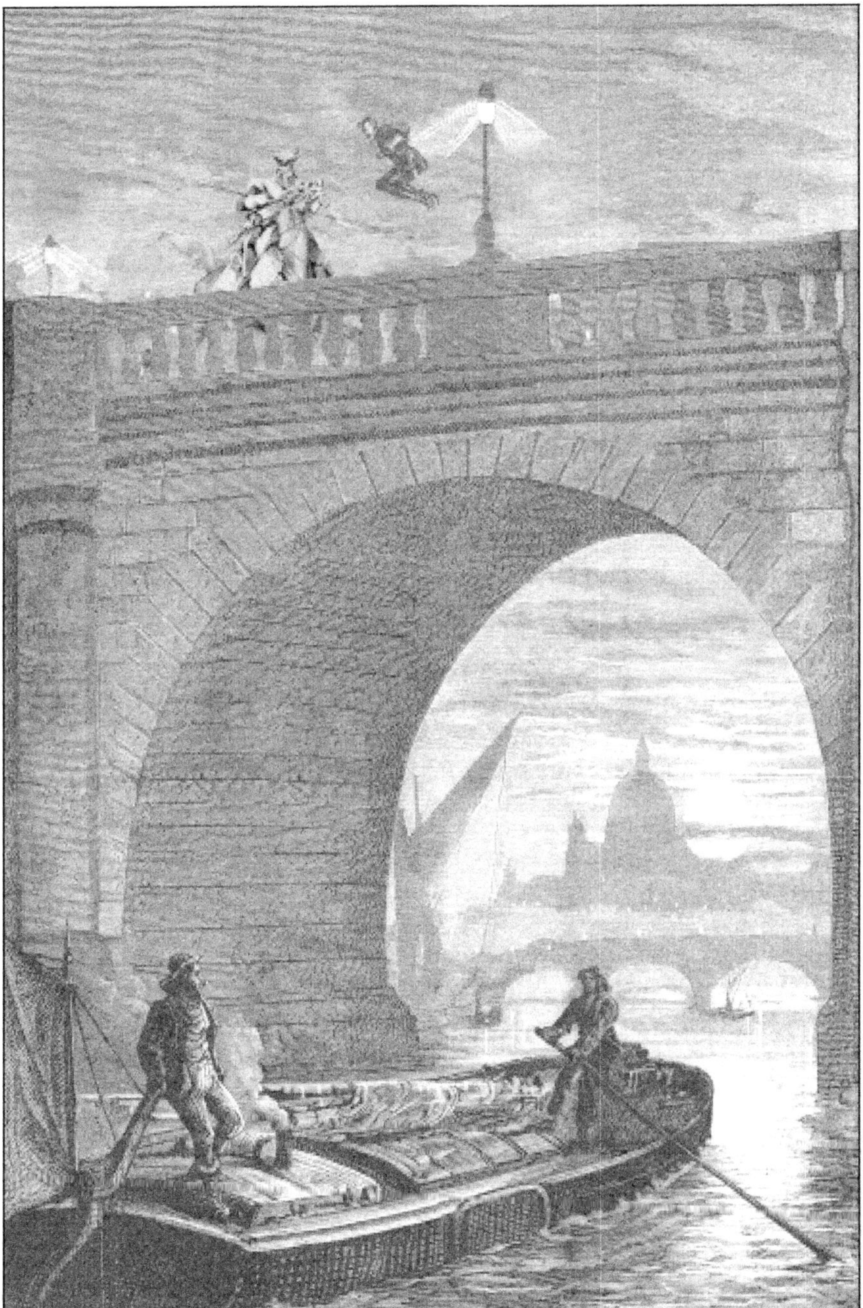

Wheeling his steed about, the Colonel took my measure and kicked into a charge, the iron point of his lance aimed squarely at my chest. I had seen this thrust pin men to the ground like butterflies. Hooves thundering, pennon snapping, cuirass flashing in the lamplight, Manfred charged, and I well recalled that my enemy had been amongst Tennyson's "six hundred" at Balaklava. He would give no quarter.

I sprang aside to the left, my only option; Manfred reined in hard, cutting about to his right. His horse was a magnificent, agile beast. We stood, poised, for an instant; then the Colonel jabbed at me with his lance, the iron spike flashing towards my face. I parried with my right arm and seized the thick bamboo shaft, bracing myself to haul him down, but he drove in, spurring the horse straight towards me and forcing me back almost to the balustrade. I leaped up and over, still gripping the lance, in hopes of disarming him, but he rode with my jump, keeping his own grip secure, and wheeled about again, driving me further back towards the rescuers.

"You have a tiger by the tail, Jack-me-lad, and you are losing ground!"

Now the Black Maria and the mounted Peelers were pulling up to a stop, their passage blocked by the wrecked coach, scarcely ten yards from where we fought. The great crowd on foot and the grey carriage were not far behind.

"Positively Shakespearean, this!" the Colonel remarked, as my spring stilts skidded over the paving stones. "But for all that you may cast yourself as the virtuous Richmond or Macduff, London sees only monstrous Caliban!"

At that, Manfred pulled back sharply on the reins and his horse reared up, lashing out with its hooves. One struck me in the shoulder, a glancing blow but enough to rip me away from the lance and knock me, spinning, off balance. The horse lunged at me again mid-spin, hooves crashing down upon the paving, and sheer luck prevented me from being crushed. As it was, I landed heavily upon my back, the breath knocked out of me; but I was still between the Colonel and the rescuers, who now cried out:

"By God, soldier, give the devil what-for!"

"Be quiet, you, and heave! Heave, I tell you!"

As I tried to recover my wind, Manfred was backing his horse three smart steps. Shifting his grip on the lance and spurring the animal into another great lunge, he thrust the weapon at my throat. I was barely able to writhe away in time and the spike struck violent sparks from the flagstones where I had lain.

Stunned, exhausted and desperate to gain breathing space, I closed my eyes and flicked the trigger on my belt. Both horse and rider recoiled at the incandescent burst; their shadows, suddenly stark and grotesquely elongated in the pressing fog, looming back behind them as the Peelers and crowd from the city surged forward to surround us.

Costers and sweeps, drabs and shipwrights, bankers and clerks and lumberers, all whose business or pleasure had brought them into the City and whose curiosity now made them witness to the downfall of Spring Heeled Jack.

Chapter 40

Manfred swung down from the saddle and drew his sabre from its sheath, pointing it directly at my chest.

"Here, London!" the Colonel boomed. "Here is the fox in your coop, brought to bay at last! Here is the devil himself abroad in the beating heart of England!"

The Peelers fanned out, forming a loose barrier line between ourselves and the pressing, fearful and fascinated crowd, as the Colonel continued:

"How many poor young girls fell sorry victim to this midnight freak, eh?"

"The soldier's right, he is," came a gruff man's voice from the crowd. "That Polly Brown in Soho … the Masterson girl …"

The crowd pushed in still closer, a hardening of righteous resolve.

"No, I were there when they found Polly Brown," a woman insisted. "Jack tried to save her! I saw it with me own two eyes!"

"But he killed …"

"He did not kill anyone!"

From behind us resounded a voice that matched the Colonel's in tone of command. The crowd parted to admit Charles and Catherine Lea, drenched, pale as phantoms, supporting each other as they staggered toward us, but alive and angry.

Two constables stepped forward to assist the clearly injured and exhausted pair, but they were waved away.

"This man … this Spring Heeled Jack … he is the hero of the hour!" Catherine proclaimed.

"And this soldier ..." Charles began, but then Manfred whirled toward him, the shining steel of his sabre describing a decapitating arc. I leapt high between them; the Colonel's sword rebounded from my spring stilt, was knocked from his hand and spun, gleaming, point over pommel, into the Thames.

Instantly thereafter, Colonel Manfred was seized by the constables.

"To the Black Maria with this scoundrel," Charles ordered. "He shall be charged with kidnapping and with attempted murder!"

Manfred did not protest as he was dragged away, but his gaze locked onto mine, speaking his heart's truth; he would gladly feed me to something after he had killed me.

"Inspector Lea," began one of the constables, a lanky chap with a mournful expression, "what of the Spring Heeled Jack? A hero he may be, Sir, but surely also a highwayman and rogue ..."

Charles and Catherine glanced regretfully at each other, and then at me. Lea was about to say something when he was interrupted:

"I can speak to that, Sir!"

Shouldering through the crowd was the familiar, bullish and bewhiskered form of Brother Vinegar Tom.

"If I might 'ave a quiet word with you, Inspector?"

Lea gestured for the big man to approach him and, together with Catherine, they spent some moments in earnest private conversation, during which several more glances were cast in my direction and, after which, Tom stepped away and melted back into the crowd. Moments later, I saw him step up into the grey carriage and shut the door.

Then Charles Lea spoke again:

"Ladies and gentlemen, City constables - I have been informed that the Spring Heeled Jack is afforded the protection of the Crown. He is to go free!"

There commenced a hubbub of confused consternation punctuated by some cheers, some boos, and the beginnings of orders from the assembled constables that all should disperse and clear the bridge, while the Leas finally consented to being helped to walk. Both were evidently close to swooning from their loss of blood and from the cold.

As the crowd, the Black Maria and mounted escorts began to turn back toward the City, I helped Charles and Catherine into Vinegar Tom's carriage.

"Guy's Hospital!" Tom shouted to the driver, rapping hard on the wall. The carriage lurched and began the complicated manoeuvre of turning about; meanwhile, blood seeped from the deep gash in Charles's back and the two neat holes through Catherine's left shoulder. As Tom and myself staunched their wounds with clean silk kerchiefs, the big man spoke quickly:

"You'll both be fine with a bit of proper care and the hospital is close by. Master Spring Heel, I reckon you'd best be away before we arrive there, for everyone's sake."

He looked to be about to say more, but instead shook his head and offered only a weary smile.

With Roland dead and Manfred apprehended, I had yet one more item of business with the Hellfire Club:

"And the matter of the estate?" I asked.

"Settled, I should say, as of this wild evening," Tom replied, "but you, Sir, will need to think 'ard on your choices, if you catch me drift."

"I have done so," I replied, and then I removed my scarlet mask.

Tom's eyes widened, but his surprise was nothing compared to the startlement of Charles and Catherine Lea.

"Mr. Haining! Jack Haining? By God …"

"My true name is Ashton. Please listen, all of you," I continued, "for we've not much time and I've much to say."

And so ended, during that short coach ride from London Bridge to Guy's Hospital, my life and fantastical "crimes" as the Spring Heeled Jack; and so began, during that same ride, the new and happy life, which now, so many years later, is drawing to its natural close.

Epilogue

I have all but completed my memoir; but a few words yet remain.

Colonel Manfred, who was the architect of so much of my personal misfortune and who had designs to enact misery on so many more, was duly tried and sentenced on criminal charges, chiefly those relating to the kidnappings and attempted murders of Charles and Catherine Lea. Suddenly leaderless, his Thuggee network had fractured into rival cliques and, although there were a few terrible retaliatory incidents - not by any means least, the assassinations of Major Dunfries and his aides in 1870 - the "Second Rebellion" that might have left the monstrous Manfred in control of British India never came to pass.

One morning in the Autumn of 1887 - the same year that Charles Lea retired, with all due honours, from his position as Inspector - I read that Colonel Manfred had died in Newgate Gaol. This news brought me nothing but a sober satisfaction. Apparently two decades of hard labour had not broken him, and he was described as a "model prisoner"; but I had known that dank and dreary place in which he suffered, and felt the dispiriting humiliation of a sunless life, forever bound by iron bars and shackles, just reward for all his perfidy.

But onward, now, to much happier and more worthy things!

The reader who has borne with my strange adventures thus far must surely wonder at how, indeed, I reclaimed my name and title. The answer is this; concomitant with the trial of Colonel Manfred, a plot of my own devising was enacted through the mysterious agencies of the Hellfire Club; and at a crucial moment of the trial, Jack Ashton himself was called to the stand as witness.

The courtroom erupted into consternation as I entered, flanked by Charles and Catherine, and the defendant started to his feet, only to be shoved down into his seat by two very burly bailiffs. But as it was subsequently explained to that court, and then reported in the newspapers the next day, Captain Jack Ashton had, in fact, never hanged. Rather than a traitor to his Queen and Country, he had been the innocent victim of a conspiracy orchestrated by none other than Colonel Manfred; a plot fortunately discovered by an honest and true (and fictional) East India Company bureaucrat.

An (equally fictional) impostor - a condemned murderer who had borne strong likeness to the rightful heir of Ashton Hall - had swung from the Newgate scaffold in his name, all were told. Meanwhile, Ashton himself was kept safe and secure until such time as the plot could be revealed and his name and reputation restored.

No mention whatsoever was made of the Leaping Demon of Soho.

I gave his mantle, springs and accoutrements to the Hellfire Club, and for all I know they hold them still, entombed in whatever grotto or vault or secret museum those shadowy gamesters may inhabit in their present incarnation. After a time, the Spring Heeled Jack receded once again in the popular memory; only a few today recall him as anything other than a tall tale told by nannies to keep their young charges safe.

I believe that this is all as it should be.

So it was that, in due course, I took up the positions that I still hold to this day. Lady Catherine and myself divide our time between Ashton Hall and our Sutton Row address, and have been much engaged in charitable works, especially the Edward Burrage Foundation, which benefits London's poorest children. Charles is, as ever, our most trusted advisor and companion, and we also enjoy a warm friendship with the suffragette Jane Sawyer - known as Jegane, when she led the Shivering Jemmies - who works with us at the Foundation, as a fierce and tireless advocate for social reform.

We have recently invested in a motorcar company; we patronise the arts and do our quiet best to improve the lot of our fellows, as best befits those of fortunate station. I like to think that my father would have approved.

Our own children - now all grown, of course - and our two grandchildren are well and fine. Though I harbour fears for the future of England - for a war with martial Germany cannot be far away - I must and do believe that their lives will be largely filled with good works.

And so it is to our sons Cecil and Geoffrey, to our daughter Isobel, her fine husband Arthur and their children Emily and little Eddie that I dedicate this memoir, that they may know something of their family's not-too-distant history. It was dark and it was colourful, both at once, and if there was sadness and danger then, I should say, no worthwhile adventure can be without those.

Should these splendid young people, upon reading my words, be tempted to draw any moral from them, let it be this:

Fay ce que voudras, my loved ones. Do as you will.

Sir John "Jack" Ashton
Ashton Hall
September 5th, 1913

About this story

I was probably about ten years old when I first came across the legend of Spring Heeled Jack, in a book of my father's surveying the long-forgotten genre of Victorian penny dreadful adventures. As a superhero-obsessed boy in the austere sociopolitical climate of mid-'70s New Zealand, I'd take all the escapism I could get.

And here, it seemed to me, was an early - perhaps the earliest? - prototype of my beloved caped crusaders. Yes, Jack had clearly first emerged as a sinister urban myth, but I learned that, by the late 19th century, generations of penny dreadful writers had transformed him from boogeyman to anti-hero to altruistic avenger.

My passion for comic book heroics diminished as I grew older, but I remained fond of the genre and interested in its history. Pop-culture historians of the 1980s and '90s, however, seldom seemed to pay Jack his due, if they were aware of him at all, preferring to date the "origin" of the superhero genre to Superman's first appearance in June of 1938. Some attention was also paid to the pulp adventurers of the 1920s - Zorro being considered a good example of a proto-Batman, with a dash of Robin Hood - but their penny dreadful and dime novel antecedents remained largely unheralded.

Before Johnston McCully introduced Zorro in *The Curse of Capistrano* (1919), however, before Russel Thorndike's Scarecrow first rode out in *Doctor Syn: A Tale of the Romney Marsh* (1915) and certainly decades before Batman, Spring Heeled Jack had set the tropes. Here was a wealthy and athletic man who, in response to personal crisis, creates an alternate identity, devising a distinctive mask and costume and an arsenal of unusual weapons. He establishes a hidden base and wages a guerrila campaign of intimidation and retribution against evildoers. He also spends an inordinate amount of time haunting rooftops. The late-Victorian rendition of Spring Heeled Jack was, for almost all intents and purposes, the very first costumed superhero.

Even today, Spring Heeled Jack is much more commonly recalled, in his early, eldritch incarnations, by folklorists and cryptozoologists rather than by comic book aficionados, though he has appeared in a scattering of comics and novels over the past several decades. I strongly recommend Karl Bell's 2012 academic anthology *The Legend of Spring-heeled Jack* to readers who take an interest in that history, as it was an invaluable resource to me in writing this story.

The Life and Fantastical "Crimes" of Spring Heeled Jack is my own tribute to the penny dreadful milieu and to Jack's unique place in the annals of superheroic fiction. Since I began writing it, I've been pleased to see the character appear in the sixth and seventh episodes of the 2015 *Jekyll and Hyde* TV series - although disappointed by his presentation as a callow youth, whose role was basically to look the part and then to be victimised by a succession of more formidable adversaries.

In the same year, though, Spring Heeled Jack appeared as a mysterious and potent villain in the *Assassin's Creed: Syndicate* video game, and then in 2016 a less visually impressive, but still gratifyingly dynamic version of Jack was featured in episode 4 of the *Houdini and Doyle* series.

Scholars of the character and lore will have observed how very fast and loose I've played with those, shuffling names, dates and events with some abandon, mixing early-mid 19th century urban myth with later fiction, etc. I hope that hasn't proved too distracting, and that you have enjoyed this tale.

Tony Wolf
Chicago, Illinois
January 2nd, 2020

Printed in Great Britain
by Amazon